There and Back

A Perdido Key Novel

by

Lori O'Gara

Copyright © 2018 by Lori O'Gara

All rights reserved.

This is a work of fiction. Names, characters, places, and incidents either are the products of the author's imagination or are used fictitiously. Any resemblance to actual persons, living or dead, businesses, companies, events, or locales is entirely coincidental.

Published in The United States of America

ISBN-13: 978-1975785536

ISBN-10: 1975785533

No part of this book may be reproduced in any form unless written permission is granted from the author or publisher. No electronic reproductions, information storage, or retrieval systems may be used or applied to any part of this book without written permission. Due to the variable conditions, materials, and individual skills, the publisher, author, and editor, disclaim any liability for loss or injury resulting from the use or interpretation of any information presented in this publication. No liability is assumed for damages resulting from the use of the information contained herein.

www.loriogara.com

Cover Copyright © 2018 by Lori O'Gara

My thanks to all the readers who love William Porter as much as I do. This book is for you.

To my husband, for keeping me safe with the shield of prayer and sword of love. You know, right?

Have I not commanded you? Be strong and of good courage; do not be afraid, nor be dismayed, for the Lord your God is with you wherever you go."

Joshua 1:9 (NKJV)

Chapter One

William Porter, a self-proclaimed sinner cowboy from the hills of Tennessee, adjusted his black felt cowboy hat, the leather band worn by age and the constant fingering of his strong fingers. His hands were not rough and calloused like an actual rancher, but soft. Nevertheless, William Porter was, at heart, a true cowboy. If he had been alive in the glory days of the west, he would have worn a white hat, not black. William possessed all the qualities of a good cowboy and a few of the black hat wearing villain, only when necessary. A cowboy always put the needs of the herd before himself. The safety of others, especially the defenseless, was of top priority for William Porter. He occasionally scoffed at the situations that he found himself involved in and tried to avoid helping others. When he attempted to walk away his conscience would not allow him to let people down. He was hard wired to sacrifice himself for the greater good. William was acutely aware that justice is best served when it is dispensed quickly and efficiently. God used William more than once as the instrument of providing that justice even though his primary philosophy was do unto others before they did unto someone innocent or weaker.

    William removed his hat, sat down at a breakfast table in a classic hotel suite, and opened a bible. He will order something to eat after he read, he thought. He had spent the last six weeks closing a property investment deal in Georgia that was not easy. He was glad to be leaving Savannah. It wasn't as difficult as the Perdido Key, Florida deal had been and there were no damsels in distress in Georgia. However, this deal had been stressful just the same. William Porter, a legendary land developer and contract closer for the renowned Chapin and Holster investment company, was no stranger to tough financial negotiations. He and Mark Alonso, his assistant and protege, had decided to take a last weekend in Savannah to relax before leaving the beautiful city. They were going to pretend to be tourists, something that they never did. Even when in Florida they did not take days just to sight-see and enjoy the local fun. William's mind drifted to the time he had spent with Krystal Sabine. Being a tourist was not what William had wanted to do in Savannah. He wanted to get back to his office in Nashville and on to the next deal. Work was what William did best. Even as the thoughts left his mind, he knew that was not entirely true. William cared about people. He loved his family and was ready to settle down. God just didn't have that in the plans for William.

God had different plans for Mark. He had plans that included one cute Florida librarian.

Mark prearranged for his girlfriend Lauren, whom he had met doing research in Pensacola for the Florida deal, to fly over to Savannah and spend the weekend with him. This arrangement left William to his own devices for the next three days. *What will I do with myself for three days?* William thought as he looked out across the river from the window in his room on the sixth floor. The hotel was situated on the edge of the historic Riverwalk district. The Georgia Queen glided across the water, its big wheel spinning as it floated by.

    William sighed, took a deep breath, looked down at the open bible and read a few passages. A verse jumped off the page at him, as they often did when he emptied his mind to the word of God; "Have I not commanded you? Be strong and courageous. Do not be afraid; do not be discouraged, for the Lord your God will be with you wherever you go." In his head, he heard a clear voice, "Go". William sighed again and spoke out loud, "Ok, Lord." William learned a long time ago, the hard way, that ignoring the call of God could be detrimental to his state of mind.

William picked up the desk phone and requested a car to pick him up. Just one more inconvenience for William caused by Mark having a woman in his life. He dressed in his signature black sports coat, black cowboy hat with its leather band, crisp white shirt, blue jeans and boots. He made his way down to the lobby and to the waiting limo. As he removed his hat, climbed into the back seat. The driver nodded and leaned down slightly.

"Where to sir?" the driver asked.

"What is your name, driver?" William asked.

"Carl."

William chuckled remembering the butler at the beach hotel named Carlos, "Ok Carl, I am starving for a good home cooked breakfast. I don't like chain restaurants so what do you recommend?"

"I agree with you. I hate chain slop halls. I would say the World Famous Clary's Café. Best breakfast in town served all day, but it's only about a mile from here. Would you would prefer to walk?" Carl said.

Looking down at his boots William said, "No thanks, I think I will ride."

"Sure thing, boss. I can see why you wouldn't want to scuff up your rhinestone cowboy boots" Carl said as he closed the door of the car shaking his head. "A cowboy in Savannah. I don't see that every day."

The car pulled up in front of Clary's in a matter of minutes. William exited the car without waiting for the chauffeur to open the door. Carl scrambled to the back of the sedan. "Man, I'm supposed to open the door."

"I will text you when I am ready for you to come pick me up, alright?" William said to Carl. The dismayed man nodded and walked back to the driver's side muttering under his breath. "Damn cowboy."

Clary's was a small light blonde brick building with a striped green and red awning spanning the font over large plate glass windows and a pine wood door. There were a few white wrought iron café style tables and chairs out front for the diner full of people eating delicious looking food. William's mouth began to water, and his stomach began to growl. He opened the door and gave his name to the waitress who led him just a few steps to a corner table. He sat down and looked at the menu. It didn't take him long to decide on Eggs Benedict Florentine which according to the menu consisted of poached eggs, and Canadian bacon on a toasted English muffin, topped with fresh sautéed spinach and hollandaise sauce, with a choice of buttered grits or potatoes. William decided on the grits.

"Hi, I'm Alison. What can I get you this fine morning?" William looked up in to green eyes twinkling over a freckle scattered small nose and a dazzling smile of dainty white teeth. Alison looked to be in her early thirties. Upon closer inspection, William could see faint, tired lines around her eyes and mouth decided that she was a bit older than she looked. William gave the pretty waitress his order of Eggs Benedict and she sat a cup of hot coffee on the table.

"How did you know I wanted coffee?" he asked her.

"You look like a coffee drinker." She grinned and walked away to give the kitchen cook the cowboy's order. William looked up from watching her walk away to see a stained-glass picture of the famous Bird Girl statue. William thought that after breakfast he would go over to the Telfair Museum and see the real thing.

Alison came out of the kitchen with hands and arms laden with plates that she skillfully balanced as she glided across the dining room floor maneuvering around tables to place the food down in front of a family of four seated at the table next to William. As she turned to walk away a petite woman about the same age as Alison approached her.

"Hi, I knew I'd find you here," the woman said.

"Hi Faith" Alison said breathlessly. "What's up?"

"You said we could look for some things for the sale" Faith said.

"Yeah that. As you can see I am working here." Alison reached up and wiped her forehead with the back of her hand. William tried not to eavesdrop, but it was near to impossible not to overhear what the two women were saying.

Alison thought, *I love her, but her timing stinks*. Out of all her friends, Alison liked Faith the most because they were completely different. It is a miracle that they were friends at all. Faith was in church every Sunday and Alison could count on one hand how many times she had been in a church of any kind in the past ten years. Faith did not date and Alison had a date every weekend, with a different guy. Well every weekend that she could get away from her teenage daughter, she considered. Alison loved to eat Chinese takeout and watch horror movies. Faith hated both. Even her friend's name implied goodness.

"Look Faith, I promised to give you some stuff for your church sale, and I will, but it has to wait till I can get off. I am swamped here," Alison said trying not to allow the annoyance she felt to seep out in her voice.

"I was afraid you would change your mind" Faith said. She did not hide any of her irritation with her hands on her hips and pouted lips. Alison winced inside. "She knows me so well," Alison said under her breath, then to Faith, "I get off work at five. Meet me at Mom's house." Alison ran back to the kitchen, picked up the order destined for William's table and spun right back out through the kitchen door.

As she hurried out of the kitchen she ran smack into Faith and dropped the perfect plate of eggs benedict florentine on to the floor where it splattered onto William's mirror polished boots. "Oh, God! I am so sorry!" she said to William as she dropped to her knees and began to wipe the oozy mess off the cowboy's boots with the towel that a fellow waitress tossed in her direction.

"Don't worry about it. Just get the cook back over the frying pan, so I don't starve to death," William laughed. Alison continued to clean up the floor as the towel wielding waitress went to inform the cook about the disaster. Faith shook her head and made her way out the front door.

Alison cleaned up the floor, picked up the plate, and got out of the way as a busboy came behind her with a mop. The busboy expertly cleaned up the last of the spill.

William motioned to the empty chair across the table from him and said to Alison, "Sit." Alison looked at the cowboy as if he spoke in a foreign language. She noticed he also had green eyes and dimples. *Oh, my goodness, dimples!* she thought.

"I...I...can't. I'm working."

"Look give it a minute. You need to regain your composure. This is strictly a self-serving offer. I do not want my second plate of food to suffer the same fate as the first. Give your brain and shaking hands a minute to catch up." William said. "If your boss gives you any grief, I'll tell him or her I told you to sit."

Alison sighed, pulled out the chair and sat down facing the handsome cowboy with the dimples. "It's her and thanks" she said and wiped her forehead again with a paper napkin laying on the table instead of the back of her hand. "I'm sorry. I'm just stretched thin right now," she said.

"I heard you talking to your friend," William said. "I am William, by the way, William Porter."

"I'm Alison Lawson. Yeah, her church is having a garage sale to raise money for a mission trip." Alison smiled. "I just don't do well around churchy people. I like them just fine. I have no filter and I can't control my mouth. The other thing is that I hate the fakeness of some of them." she said matter of fact to William.

"I understand that. I'm Christian and I do not like fake churchy people either." William said with a smirk. "Not all Christians are that way though, Alison"

"I know," Alison was certain that there wasn't one fake thing about William Porter. She looked over at the hostess who was giving her a sideways glance that screamed, *what do you think you are doing sitting down at a table talking with a customer?*

"Thanks for the chat but I have to work." She went back to waiting on tables.

William Porter was sure there was more to this woman than meets the eye as he watched her walk away. His own eyes dropped to stare at the feminine sway in her hips.

Chapter Two

After Alison got off work she and Faith sifted through possible items for the charity sale. The two women groped through the attic of Alison's parents' house on a mission to find anything that may catch a dollar. There were countless boxes of dusty clothes, books, dishes, and other long forgotten treasures that must have been important enough at one time for someone to heave up to the attic. Across the far side of the grimy room, there was a huge trunk. Alison tried to push open the lid, but it was locked. "Shit" she said.

"Allie, language! You are a potty mouth. Ladies don't need to use words like that." Faith reminded Alison every time she used a colorful word that it was not lady like to use profanity.

"Yeah yeah, do you see a lady here? What about a key, see a key anywhere?" Alison said.

"No, I wouldn't begin to know where to look." Faith stood in the middle of the room looking around. The dust swirled around her head like a halo. Alison grunted as she turned away from her friend. Even in the dirty attic, Faith looks angelic.

"It's just a bunch of junk anyway." Alison managed to find a few things that may bring a couple of bucks. She put a ceramic cat, a corkscrew that looked antique, a lamp, and a painting of a mountain on black velvet in to an empty box.

"You know what they say about one man's junk." Faith said and asked, "You are going to be there tomorrow?"

"Yeah, I have to be there, I promised" Alison replied with no enthusiasm.

"Right," Faith smiled another perfect smile. "You did. You'll have fun Allie. There will be new people for you to meet and some folks you know." Alison knew who Faith meant. She was talking about the exasperating guy she introduced to Alison last year at a street party on the Fourth of July. He was so cute but nosey. He wanted Alison to tell him about her family. Family was one topic Alison could do without talking about.

"I will be there, but I am not making any promises to be friendly" Alison grunted. Faith laughed at her friend. She knew that Alison would be on her best behavior. She was not an outgoing social girl, but she was never intentionally rude in mixed company. Faith said a silent prayer for Alison as she gathered up the box of newfound yard sale products.

"Whatever you say. I know you will be fine. Besides there will be free food. You can always help cook hamburgers or fries" Faith said jokingly.

"Um…. no." Alison disliked being around churchy people, but she hated cooking even worse. "I have no problem selling junk to old ladies. I will stay at the table guarding your cash box, but I am not cooking for a bunch of bible thumpers."

"Sure thing, I will see you tomorrow. Don't stay out too late, will ya? I will see you at seven, ok?" Faith said as she started to leave, and Alison walked her out.

Alison began to protest. "Seven, in the morning, are you nuts? I hate getting up early on my days off."

"Yes, seven, we have to go through all the stuff, price it and organize it" Faith said, "You promised." Her singsong voice trailing behind her as she climbed into a gleaming red sports car. Just another reminder to Alison that Faith's life was perfect and her life was not even close. "I can be sick!" Alison shouted at her friend's car as it pulled away from the curb.

A little while later back at her house, Alison reached in her closet for a pink satin halter and a black pair of slacks. She wanted to dance the stress away and Ollie's was just the place. The local joint was full of good-looking nobodies that would buy her a drink for a smile and a flash of her long eye lashes. She could dance and be just the pretty girl that all the guys want to take home. She slipped on a pair of black stilettos and looked at herself in the full-length mirror.

Too bad I didn't get that sexy cowboy's number, Alison thought. She considered calling Hank. He was always willing to have a good time and he was infatuated with her. She decided against it and chose rather to go it alone. It was always fun to be single and free. It was a game for Alison to see how many offers she could get in one night. One weekend last month, she got four guys to ask her if they could take her home. She could not choose just one, so she stumbled out to a cab unaccompanied.

There was no way Alison could convince Faith to go to a bar. Faith with her perfect body, smile, and life, she could have her pick of men. Faith was waiting for the one God would send her. Alison had told her good luck with that. God doesn't care who we are with, what we do with our lives or any other thing we do. He has better things to worry about, like all the starving children in Africa for Christ sake.

Alison looked in on her daughter who was laying across her bed watching a movie. "Lights out at eleven, got it?"

"Yes mom" the teen said.

"I am locking the door behind me, no company. You hear me?" Alison said.

"Yes mom" said the girl again as if on auto reply.

Ollie's was crowded and smoky when Alison walked into the place. She found an empty stool at her usual end of the long oak bar. Casey and Holly were on the dance floor giving the room a show. Casey, a tall blonde wrapped her arms around Holly's waist and turned her around. Casey rubbed Holly's backside with one hand and reached around to hold her breast in the other. Alison knew that they were drunk already. Holly's long dark hair was in a clip that she grabbed and released with a dramatic shake of her head. Her silky midnight dark hair cascaded down her back.

Several men who were watching the girls shouted at them. "Kiss her!" yells a frizzy headed man with bigger earrings than Alison's gold hoops. Holly grabbed Casey and planted a big sloppy kiss on her lips. Alison ignored them and called to the bartender to bring her a drink.

"Hey Al, the usual?" the bartender called to her. Dave was in his forties and his wife Olive is at least five years younger than he was. He bought the bar for his wife as a wedding gift fifteen years ago. He was a stocky man with a warm brotherly personality. "Your girls are in rare form tonight."

"Yeah I see that" Alison looked back at the girls on the dance floor just in time to see Holly flash the audience her milky white bare breasts. "Great…Dave would you call Holly's brother to come get these two? I just can't handle them tonight."

"All ready on it, Darlin" Dave said as he handed Alison a Cosmopolitan in a martini glass. Alison liked to dance and drink, but there was no way she was going to embarrass herself as her girlfriends were doing. She wished she had called Hank after all. At least then, she would have some intelligent conversation. Her idea of spending the evening with her girls measuring up the guys in the club and comparing them to one another was not going to happen with the Gibson girls. Holly and her cousin Casey were falling over drunk and it wasn't even eight o'clock. Alison loved to play, but there was a limit to what she would do in public.

She downed the Cosmo and ordered a scotch neat. Grandpa Jack would be proud she thought. Alison didn't usually mix her alcohol but considering that Mr. Gibson would walk into Ollie's any minute she knew she would need the support of liquid courage to be polite to him. Polite hell. I will need it to breathe, she thought.

As if on cue, the front door opened to Lance Gibson in all his glory. "Hell, he even has a halo. What the fuck?" Alison said under her breath as she noticed the way the street light shone in on his gleaming dark hair. He was standing in a black Armani suit, crisp white shirt, missing a tie, classic. He was looking hot as ever from that halo down to his polished wing tips. Alison had to look away.

"Hi Allie"

"Hello Lance"

"The girls are being their normal unruly selves I see." He said and took the bar stool on her right. Alison's hands were shaking so she sat on them, a habit she formed shortly after first meeting Lance Gibson. The only problem was that she needed her scotch that Dave sat in front of her. She risked one quivering hand to reach for her glass and took another sip of her drink to drown the past eighteen years of memories that were beginning to flood her brain. "Yeah they are, that's why I had Dave call you." She managed to speak one sentence with no shake in her voice and that was a stroke of luck. She didn't attempt any more word. Drink she told herself. Dave reappeared asking Lance what he could get him, "The usual Mr. Gibson?"

"Thanks Dave, but no, I am only going to be here long enough to load the girls into the limo. How about an H20 and lime?" Alison was gazing at Lance through the mirror behind the bar and suddenly realized he was staring at her profile. "So, Alison what's new with you?"

"You know, dealing with the death of a family member has me busy." Alison said.

"I can imagine. Sorry about your dad" Lance said.

"You have no idea." Alison whispered as she swallowed hard.

She and Lance Gibson were never good with small talk. It was almost painful watching his eyes flicker as he tried to think of something polite to say. He was staring at her again. "How are you really, love?" He leaned into her. Almost forehead to forehead, she closed her eyes and did not answer his question.

The air was sucked away from around them like when an approaching hurricane was in the Atlantic. The electricity between them was almost visible. They could have been talking about the weather, latest sale at the Piggly Wiggly, or the score from the last college football game and the atmosphere would be the same high charged storm. It was identical every time they were in sight of each other. Lance looked up briefly and nodded at Sam, his driver who had been standing discreetly in a dark corner.

Alison sighed and relaxed a bit, thankful for the distraction to break the spell. Sam went directly to the bouncer. They both then went to the dance floor to collect the troublemakers.

Alison risked looking directly into Lance's blue eyes and her stomach took flight with swarms of butterflies. "Ugh" she said as she downed the rest of the scotch. Lance reached over and lightly placed his hand on her knee. She immediately thought thank God, I didn't wear a dress, but the effect was the same as if he had touched her bare skin. A bolt of energy shot up her leg to her most private area and proceeded up to her heart as he traced small circles around her kneecap. Lance moved into her again and whispered, "I miss seeing you Alison."

"Don't, just don't" was all she could risk saying. She waved subtly to Dave who brought her a second scotch, a double. She mouthed thank you to Dave and he winked at her. One thing Dave knew was how to read people and he had been reading these two for years. This was not new; they had been standing in this fire many times before.

Lance stood adjusting his suit jacket and inclined to place his lips close to her ear. Alison could feel the rough day-old stubble of his cheek next to hers. She drank in the scent that was him. She felt the exact feeling, all these years, the same response of her body when he touched her and the same ache in her heart that plagued her.

"I know, my sweet, this is a dangerous game we play. I know we can't, but that doesn't stop me from wanting you. Missing you." His words slink into her ear like a mist on the shore kindled with summer heat. Alison looked up at his back in the mirror behind the bar and whispered, "One of us always gets burned Lance, and it is usually me."

Lance moved away from her and took a step toward the door. Suddenly Alison found her voice. "Tell the wife hello for me, won't you Lance." She saw his shoulders slump slightly as he paused for a second and then Lance Gibson walked out of Ollie's. She instantly regretted that she could turn from soft hot to hard cold ice so quickly.

Chapter Three

Alison groaned as the alarm blared. She managed to shower and dress just as Faith honked her horn outside. Alison looked at her teenage daughter who was sleeping sprawled across the bed in much the same way as she was the night before. Instead of waking her, Alison left a note. She climbed in to her friend's car and pushed her sunglasses back up on her nose.

"Good morning." Faith croons and Alison moaned.

"Shhhh not so loud." Alison begged

"Coffee" Faith said and handed a cup to Alison. "You went out, didn't you?"

"Yes, and he was there." Alison confessed.

"Oh, Allie." Faith said, and they rode in silence the rest of the way to the church. Faith knew it was not the time to preach the dangers of Lance Gibson to her friend.

The parking lot was full of tables loaded with other people's yard sale paraphernalia. At the far end was a huge grill just starting to smoke. The smell of the grill turned Alison's stomach as she stood up out of the sports car. Faith pulled the box of stuff they had rescued from the attic out of the car and motioned to Alison to pick up a bag full of other items. A woman in denim overalls approached Faith and Alison. She and Faith exchange words as Alison avoided eye contact with the woman and the other volunteers milling around her by ducking her head behind the sunglasses.

"Allie, you get to sit over there and man the book table. Should be easy for you." Faith said and pointed to a table.

"I can do that." Alison said and took a seat in a folding chair behind a large stack of paperback novels. The hours were long and slowly passed, but luckily the books sold themselves. She didn't have to do much talking. Alison flipped through a couple of romance novels and giggled wondering which one of these good pew sitters donated these gems. She picked up one with a cover splayed with a bare-chested hunk of a man with long flowing blond hair on a horse. The title was, "Warrior of the Night."

"How much for that one?" A small blue gray-haired woman reached for the book and took it from Alison's hand. "Oh, he's pretty" the woman said. Alison couldn't help but laugh out loud. "What? Just because I am old doesn't mean I can't appreciate a handsome man dearie" the woman said and picked up three more similar paperbacks. The lady shoved a five-dollar bill into Alison's hand. "Nothing wrong with a little fantasy missy." And with that the little old lady walked away.

Alison decided to take what the sweet elderly lady said to heart. She settled down in to a chair, picked up a romance novel, and began to read. Before long she dozed off. A bit later she was startled awake when her cell phone rang. It was the café. Alison answered it which was something she never did on her day off but getting called to go to work seemed a better prospect than sitting at the table selling romance novels to little old church ladies offering advice on men.

"Hi Fran. Need me to come in?" Alison said. Fran told her that the she was two waitresses short. Alison said she would be there as soon as possible. The restaurant wasn't full, but Fran was worried it would get busier later in the day. Alison waved Faith over to the table. "I have to go to work." She explained pointing to the phone in her hand. Faith frowned but nodded. "Fran be there in thirty." Saved by work, Alison thought. Relief and guilt washed over her.

~~~~~~~~

Mark pulled up to the airport and got out of the car. He wished that Lauren had allowed him to park and go in to the airport to get her. He waited on the sidewalk just like she had asked him to do as she walked out pulling her roll along luggage behind her. She was pushing her wild brown bouncy curls off her face when she saw Mark. She ran to him and threw her arms about his neck. They embraced and kissed for a few seconds. To any stranger looking at these two people greet each other they would have thought that they looked like they did not belong together. Mark was tall and brawny while Lauren was small and nerdy. He picked her up and spun her around. "How was your flight?" he asked.

"Great, how are you? How is William?" She asked.

"You know William. He is not liking having a few days with no work. I half expected him to go to Florida." Mark said.

"That would have been funny. We could have met in the airport." Lauren laughed.

Mark drove Lauren back to the hotel. They were staying in the same hotel as William. The couple was standing in the lobby waiting for Lauren to get her key to her room when William Porter walked in and smiled at her. "Hi Lauren." William said. "How is my favorite librarian? You look great."

"Thanks, you don't look so bad yourself" She answered.

"Listen I know you are not working this weekend, but how hard is it to find out basic facts about a person? I mean find out if someone is married, has kids, went to college, demographic sort of information, can you help with that?" William asked Lauren. Mark looked at his boss a bit annoyed and William ignored it.

"Sure, who are we looking to help this time?" she asked William.

"Why do you think I am helping someone?" he asked her.

"William Porter, because that is what you do." She laughed.

"No one to help. I am interested in discovering all I can about a girl I met. Let's just say she was intriguing." William said sheepishly.

"Um hum" Lauren said.

Mark smiled then. There was the William Porter he knew but had not seen in a long time. Florida had changed him, William was different. When in Florida, William had not only suffered attacks on his sobriety but his vow to God was challenged as well. The loss of love left its marks on him.

Years ago, William Porter was a lady's man. He was always seen with a drink in his hand and a pretty girl on his arm. After a woman had used him to gain company secrets, stole the deal of the century from him as he slept with her and shattered his heart, he had given his life to God. In the aftermath of his destruction, William promised God that he would never get drunk again and he would not sleep with a woman unless that woman became his wife. William came close to braking that promise when he met a beautiful jeweler and land owner. However, the Florida girl was already in love with someone else.

"Ok, I will see what I can do." Lauren said. "What's her name?"

"Alison Lawson. She works at Clary's Café." William said. The concierge handed Lauren her hotel key card. Mark and Lauren said good bye to William and headed off to their room.

William decided to go over to the café for an early lunch. He entered the dining room and asked to be seated in the same table as before. He looked around and did not see Alison. Then he remembered she was at the church rummage sale. He scolded himself for not finding out what church she was helping at. The room was not as full or as busy as the morning he was there the first time. Over in a corner was a waitress reading the newspaper and another waitress came to his table.

"Hi, my name is Fran, what can I get you sir?" she asked. Just then a blast of wind came in as the door opened and Alison came in to the restaurant in a rush. She was moving fast as she passed William's table. She said to Fran, "He takes coffee, cream and sugar." Fran and William both looked at her in surprise. "I will wait to order and for Alison to serve me once she gets settled in. If that's ok?" William said.

"Fine whatever." Fran said. Alison went to the back breakroom dropped her things off and grabbed an apron. She emerged in the dining room tying the apron around her waist.

Fran made her way over to Alison and whispered something to her. Both woman looked over at William who smiled and tipped his hat. Alison walked over to his table. "So, you asked for me huh?" Alison asked.

"Yes." William said directly. "I am surprised to see you here. Did you get kicked out of the rummage sale for using profanity in front of the pastor?"

"Nope. I sold granny porn to real grannies though. I was saved by the all mighty dollar and lazy coworkers not showing up for work. What can I get you?" she said.

"Well first I will take two eggs over easy, grits and bacon. Then I will take a yes to a dinner date with me." William said and smiled at Alison who blushed.

"I can't date customers" Alison said as she looked over at her manager who was eyeing her from across the room. "however, if you happen to come to this other place around eight tonight" she said as she scribbled something on a piece of paper "and happen to ask me out then, I might say yes." She smiled.

Alison handed him a note pad that had an auto parts store logo on it with a scrawled address. William looked at the note; his forehead furrowed.

"My other job." She explained.

"I see." He answered.

"Yeah, I'm a single mom. Anyway, let me go put your order in." Alison smiled and walked away.

That evening William gave the hotel driver the address that Alison had jotted down on the scrap of paper.

"Are you sure?" Carl asked.

"Yes, I'm sure." William answered a bit irritated.

"Ok, buddy, it's your funeral." The driver said and closed the back door of the car.

They drove about ten miles and William noticed that the homes and business began to look run down. No wonder the driver questioned him. From what William could tell by what he saw out the window of the car they were not on a good side of Savannah. Why would someone as sweet as Alison work on a street like this? William thought as the car came to a stop outside an automotive parts store. William opened the door and motioned to Carl to get back in the car. "Wait here."

"But it is my job to open doors, not just drive your no walking cowboy boots around town." Carl said exasperated.

"I said wait here." William strode into the store to see Alison sitting on a stool behind the counter tapping away on a computer with a corded land-line telephone wedged between her head and shoulder.

"We can have the alternator here in two days. Yes sir. Thank you. Good bye." She said to the person on the other end of the line. She looked up and saw William standing in front of her.

"Hi" she smiled.

"Hi, now can I have that yes?" William said.

"Yes, but I don't get off until nine. Then I should go home and check on my daughter. She is sixteen." Alison said.

"There is no way you have a daughter that old. You are too young." William protested.

"Yeah, well I got pregnant right after high school, but I am still young at heart." She said.

William did the math. He figured she was in her early thirties. She was younger than any other woman he had dated in the last few years. Still, she was stunning, and William had promised Mark that he would try to get out of this rut he had been in since Florida. That rut had been a long hard one and he supposed it was time to get out of it. "Well, we all have our burdens. Seems you are doing well for yourself. What do you do here?" he asked.

"Sell car parts and deliver to garages." She said. "I like it. My dad taught me a lot about cars. I can change a fuel pump, brakes and other stuff. It is different here from the café, different customers. I do like the café too."

"This neighborhood seems, I don't know, unsavory" he said trying not to offend her. Alison laughed. "It's not bad just older and not filled with as much money as the downtown tourist areas. I live about a mile from here."

"Give me your address and I will pick you up about nine thirty." William said. Alison wrote down her address and cell number then handed it to him. "What is this number seven?" he asked looking at the same scratchy handwriting from the note this morning. "Lot seven, it's a mobile home park" she said.

"Here is my number" he told her his cell number as she wrote it down. William put his hat back on his head and tapped it. "Call me when you are ready to go out. See you later Alison." He said.

"Bye and call me Allie. All my friends do." She smiled as she picked up a ringing telephone from the counter.

Chapter Four

Mark and Lauren walked down Savannah's famous river walk past the shops. The air was filled with a sweet smell of chocolate and caramel. They made their way to the praline store where a master candy maker was mixing a huge copper pot of caramel. "Oh, let's go in Mark." Lauren said her mouthwatering at the sweet aroma coming from the open store front.

  Mark took her hand and lead her into the candy shop. The original Savannah's Candy Kitchen store on River Street was filled to the brim with the best candies, cakes, and confections in the South. The sights and sounds were overwhelming, but Lauren was in heaven. She closed her eyes and took a deep breath. Her sweet tooth screamed for a bite.

"This smell is intoxicating. I can feel myself getting fat just breathing it in." Lauren said with a giggle.

Mark laughed too and went to the counter. He ordered a mixed box of pralines, divinity, and fudge. He turned to find Lauren accepting a chocolate turtle sample from a confectioner. She slowly let the candy melt in her mouth and closed her eyes fully immersed in the experience. Mark couldn't stand it any longer. He strode over and kissed the chocolate off her lips. "Let's go back to our room." He said in a whisper. Lauren smiled. "Not yet. Let's walk a bit further." Mark groaned, but nodded.

They continued down the river walk past the shops and entered a few. They purchased a couple of bottles of wine from a premier winery and Lauren found a brilliant purple silk scarf in a dress shop that she could not live without. The day wore on and they decided to stop for lunch. They went in to Vick's on the River. It was a fine dining restaurant in a nineteenth century warehouse.

Mark gazed across the table at Lauren. He was surprised at how much he loved this girl. In all his years, he was never attracted to the intellectual type. He was more into the physical type. His last two girlfriends, if you could call them that, were both police women. The one before that was in the Army. He never held a relationship for long. As he always put his employment for William Porter and his responsibilities first even as a priority over his love life. Lauren was different. His feelings for her were unlike any he had in the past. It helped that William liked her too. Mark smiled, then again William liked most woman.

Lauren smiled back at Mark. He reached up and pushed a strand of her dark hair off her face. She is beautiful, he thought, in a girl next door kind of way. Sweet and innocent. He felt his face flush. Well, not so innocent in the bedroom and Mark had no vow to God to worry about. Lauren saw his face and knew instantly what he was thinking about. She waved at the waiter and asked for the check.

Mark and Lauren barely made into the hotel room before they were tearing at each other's clothing. In a matter of seconds, they were completely undressed. Mark took control of the circumstances and moved her to sit on the sofa. He stood over her, his feet on the cushions and his hands on the wall above her head. His stunning erect male anatomy eye level with her. She stroked it lightly thinking that is was the most beautiful piece of manhood she had ever seen or touched. Slowly and purposely she took the head of it in to her mouth circling it with her lips. He softly moaned and whispered, "oh yes". His words giving her the push she needed to continue with her tongue.

She enveloped him with her mouth and continued to work his shaft as he moved his hips in rhythm with her. She drove her tongue down the length of him, setting off another shattering groan that escaped him that was music to her ears. He was an exquisite instrument to play, so finely tuned, and if she touched him right, he made the most glorious sounds. He grabbed her hair, yanked and pulled her closer. When she lifted her eyes, she saw that he was dissolved with pleasure. At first, he made no motion. He was quivering in her hand tormented with desire. She kept moving until he begged her to stop.

    Once he caught his breath, he moved her on to her hands and knees on the floor. Not caring that the tile pushed in to his knees as he thrust inside her. He shifted his body hitting her in the spot that turned her moans into one long sigh. She trembled against him, her legs quaking. He turned her over and continued to pleasure her. When he finally slowed and opened his eyes to look at her, he saw her hair was a rough tumble, and her face was glowing.

    They collapsed together and lay in silence for several minutes before he took her hand, guided her to the bed where he covered her gently with the quilt. She fell asleep the moment she closed her eyes.

Chapter Five

Music was blaring from inside her house as Alison got out of her car. The noise came from the end where her daughter's room was located. Shaking her head, Alison walked in to her mobile home and looked around at the laundry covering the sofa. She began to pick it up and noticed a half empty pizza box, two empty soda cans and dirty paper plates on the end table. Alison sighed. She thought about yelling for her daughter, Cara, but she knew the girl would not respond over the loud music that was shaking the floorboards. She walked down the hallway and knocked on Cara's bedroom door. Not waiting for an answer Alison opened the door.

There was a scrambling of movement of arms, legs and clothes flying as Cara and her boyfriend untangled themselves from each other. Alison waited for them to stop moving. She folded her arms over her chest and stood in the doorway. "Mom, we were just." Cara stood tall. Her dark hair a wild mess and her eyes wide as she stared at her mother. "Listen, get yourselves together and meet me in the kitchen." Alison said and walked out of the room calmly, too calmly thought Cara.

A few seconds later the two embarrassed teens were in Alison's bright yellow kitchen. Alison was talking on her phone. She called William and told him she couldn't go to dinner. She explained what she had come home too.

"Listen, you and your daughter still have to eat. Tell her to get some jeans on and I will take you both to dinner. I am already almost to your place anyway. Should be fun." William said. Alison groaned, "Fun? I doubt that." Against her better judgement, she agreed to go. Alison disconnected the call, turned and looked over at the two kids who would not look her in the eye.

"We need to get one thing straight. I am not mad, but disappointed. Please tell me you two haven't had sex yet or at least were smart about it?"

"Mom!" Cara said. Alison looked at Cara and back to the boy. He was shaking his head. "No, Ms. Alison, no sex yet. We were just messing around."

Alison felt the relief wash over her. The last thing she wanted was a grandchild to raise. She shook her head. "We will talk about this later, right now we have some place to go. Tell Noah goodbye and get dressed. Please wear something decent ok? Noah, I am not done with you. We will continue this later."

"Yes mam" the boy answered. "Bye Cara." He walked out the back door and Cara stomped out of the room. She slammed her bedroom door.

Alison ignored the display of anger and went to her room to freshen up. She changed into a pair of jeans and purple blouse. After she brushed her pony tail until her hair glistened, fixed her makeup and applied light pink lipstick she went to Cara's room. The girl was dressed in jeans too and a black t-shirt.

"Where are we going?" she asked flipping her waist length hair over one shoulder.

"A friend of mine has invited us to dinner. Well not a friend, really, we just met. Anyway, he is nice, so we will have fun getting to know him together. Consider yourself a chaperone." Alison laughed.

Cara groaned. "Mother, really? On a date? I don't want to be the third wheeled thing"

"Not a date, we just met. Dinner with a friend that is all." Alison said as she heard a knock at the front door. "Be nice and let's have a good time, ok?"

Alison went to the door with a sulking Cara on her heels. She opened the door where William stood with his hat in his hands. His hair was slicked back, and he was smiling. Damn, he is hot, Alison thought looking at William dressed in a button-down shirt in an interesting shade of blue. Not a sky blue and not a turquoise. Aqua, Alison decided.

Cara come up behind her. She looked past her mother and William to the limo that was filling the space next to Alison's humble older sedan. The chauffeur was standing at the ready next to the open back passenger door. "Is that your car?" Cara said

"Yes, well no it belongs to the hotel car service where I am staying." William said. "Hi I am William and you must be Cara?" He extends his hand.

Cara blushed. "Hi" she said as she took his hand. She shook his hand lightly and quickly. Then she bounced down the front steps to the car.

Alison locked her front door. She and William followed Cara who was already in the back seat opening compartments and flipping lights on and off. "Miss do you mind not touching every switch in the car. If you need something I am here for you." Carl said trying not to sound annoyed. Cara blushed and sat back in the seat. "There you are miss." Carl said as he moved out of the way of the door as Alison approached. Alison slid in and Cara jumped to the seat across from her mother. Carl closed the door and mumbled under his breath, "What is it with teenagers not having proper home training these days?"

William leaned in, "I am not from around here, where to girls?" he asked grinning. "Do you like Italian?" Cara asked before Alison could gather her thoughts. She was still in shock over the limo in her driveway and the gorgeous cowboy that rode up in it.

"Sure" William answered.

"There is a good place not far from here. You guys can get pasta if you want but they have awesome pizza." Cara said.

Alison shook her head, "This child will eat pizza every day all day for every meal if I let her."

"If your mom says it's ok" William said.

Alison nods and Cara tells Carl to take them to Marcello's.

Alison is amazed that the teenager who is never friendly to anyone and even less friendly to her mother's dates was being polite. Not only was she being well-mannered, but she was chatting with William. Alison was glad that William had agreed for Cara to come with them. It took the pressure off her to keep the conversation going. The silences were always the awkward part of first dates. Alison shook her head again, this is not a date, she thought. It was just dinner.

The restaurant was not crowded so they managed to get a table when they arrived. Along the right wall was a bar and to the left was an open dining room. The wall was lined with tall wide booths with black leather seats. The backs of the seats almost touched the ceiling. It made for romantic dinner dates for couples and confinement for families with small children.

There was a mixture of both types of customers seated at the tables. Cara slid in first. Then Alison in next to her. William sat across from them as the hostess lit the candles on the table and handed the trio menus to read.

"What's good here?" William asked looking at Alison, but Cara answered. "Well like I said the pizza is great but so is the pasta. They have authentic Italian dishes. I heard that the chef was born in Naples and has only been here a couple of years. Before that his grandmother was the one who opened this restaurant. They say her ghost still hangs around haunting the place."

"Oh, Cara, really?" Alison said. Cara shrugged.

"I like the portabella ravioli" Alison said. "and she likes red wine." Cara added.
"Oh, really?" William questioned.

"Yeah, her favorite is Apothic Inferno." Cara added. Alison looked at her daughter trying to figure out who the heck she was and where was her moody teenager who complains every time they go out that her mother is going to be an alcoholic if she doesn't stop drinking so much wine. What Cara doesn't know was that her mother's favorite wine was her favorite because it is aged in cured whisky barrels.

"I like red wine too, but I am not much of a drinker." William said.

The waitress came to the table and they ordered their dinner. William took Alison's recommendation and ordered the ravioli. Cara order a pizza with "everything but dead fish" she said. William then ordered a bottle of Alison's favorite red wine and a virgin bloody Mary. No vodka, extra lemon juice and olives instead. Cara made a face, "What's the point?" "Cara, don't be rude." Alison chastised. William laughed a deep belly laugh. "I get funny looks all the time from bartenders. I don't drink booze, so I make up drinks as I go. My friend in Florida got me started on Blood Mary's."

"Why don't you like booze?" Cara asked. Alison was secretly glad that her daughter had asked the question. She was also mortified that her daughter asked the grown man why he doesn't drink. "I gave my life to God a few years back and it was one of the promises I made to Him." William said plainly. Alison's heart sank. William Porter, the sexy cowboy was one of the real churchy people she avoided.

"I see." Cara said. Now Alison was completely in shock. Her daughter was the most vocal person against religion that Alison knew. It wasn't that she didn't believe in God, she did. She and Alison both didn't think God cared about people. Alison watched Cara's face as she gave what William said some thought. Any second now, she will have something negative and challenging to say to William. "I am not sure God really spends much time caring about to us." Cara said. There it is, thought Alison. "Why do you think that?" William asked.

"Not a good idea William. You just met us, and I don't think you are ready for one of Cara's tangents about how God made the earth but could care less about what we do on it." Alison said.

"Ok, since we just met" William said "we can save this discussion for another time. Tell me about school instead Cara, what is your favorite class?" William deflected. Cara shot her mother a look but sighed, "I like English Lit because I love to read." With that William and Cara spent the next several minutes discussing the latest books on the best seller list and the classics. Alison was lucky to get a word in about every other title.

The conversation stayed light and they all had a good time getting to know each other. William reached over and touched Alison's hand a few times conveying that he was genuinely interested in what she had to say. He even told Cara to give her mother a chance to speak. Cara blushed but stopped talking long enough to let

Alison give her opinion of the latest Stephen King novel.

The food was slow to arrive and suddenly Cara grabbed Alison's hand, "Mom show me where the restroom is please."

"Wait, what? You know where it is." Alison looked at her daughter.

"No, I forgot, come with me. We will be right back William excuse us." Cara said.

Cara drug her mother by the hand into the ladies' restroom. As soon as the door was closed she started in on her mother. "What are you doing? Mr. Porter is flirting with you and you are ignoring it. He is super-hot mom and if you haven't noticed he is rich. Maybe even Telfair rich." Cara said.

"Cara, I don't know this man. I just met him remember. Plus, I haven't dated, really dated in a long time." Aliso said.

"I know mom since that creep Hank with the crazy tattoos. William, Mr. Porter is nice. Give him a chance. I like him." Cara said.

Alison was astounded that her daughter who really doesn't like any adults just confessed to liking this stranger. She was sure it was the money and cowboy hat that had Cara smitten. "I see, so you are ok with me dating again all of a sudden?" Alison asked.

"If it is the rich cowboy I am." Cara grinned.

"Let's go, I bet our food is getting cold." Alison said.

The ladies made their way to the table just as the waitress sat down the food. William removed his black hat and cleared his throat. "You are not gonna pray are you Mr. Porter?'" Cara asked.

"Well actually I was, but silently." He said bowing his head.

"No, out loud." Alison said. William smiled and reached across the table taking both Alison's and Cara's hands.

William prayed a short grace thanking God for the meal and the company of two beautiful women. Alison and Cara both flushed. Alison's brain was broken at Cara's out of character behavior.

As they enjoyed the meal, Cara told them about her new writing teacher who looked like Harrison Ford. "Harrison Ford, really?" Alison said.

"Yeah, older and hot. In an adventurer sort of way. He is ragged looking. Shirt untucked, messy hair and no tie. Not stiff like the other teachers. All leather satchel and unorganized. Like a scattered professor." Cara said. "Not slick and polished like you Mr. Porter."

"Cara, please and the last thing I am is polished. I am just a normal guy. I have plenty of scattered and unorganized things in my life, trust me." William said.

"You don't seem to have a disorderly life." Alison said.

"No not at all." Cara agreed.

Just as they were about to finish desert of Tiramisu and coffee. Alison's phone went off. "I have to take this." She said excusing herself from the table. After a few short minutes, she returned. "I am so sorry. It was my mother."

"Is she alright?" William asked.
"Yes, long story she is having trouble with her house." Alison said.

"What kind of trouble? That is sort of what I do, help people with houses." William said.

"There isn't anything really that anyone can do" Alison said smiling. She was not in the mood to talk about her mother's situation and ruin the nice night they were all enjoying.

William was intrigued. He wanted to know what clouded her eyes. In the hope that he could get Alison to talk, William asked if they would like to go to the river walk. Cara used the opportunity to convince her mother to have the driver drop her off at home. She promised to conduct herself like a southern lady should and not have any boys over.

"I don't think so. Let's make it another night." Alison said. "How long are you visiting Georgia, William?"

"I understand, Alison, it is late, and you worked all day on your feet. I will be here a few more days. Actually, I can stay as long as I like, I was planning on leaving Tuesday, but my calendar is light at the moment." William answered.

William looked over at Alison who was sitting next to him. He had the urge to kiss her. If it wasn't for the teen girl sitting in the limo with them he would have already kissed her hard and more than once. Somehow from the conversations and other things he picked up on William got the feeling that Cara would approve.

They reached the mobile home park and he got out of the car reaching to give Alison his hand. Cara bounced out of the opposite side running around the car flinging her arms around a surprised William. Carl took a step back as held on to the open door. He shook his head. Teenagers were a mystery to him. Women in general were enigmas, but young ones were impossible to understand.

"Thank you, Mr. Porter, it was a lovely evening." Cara said.

"You are welcome, and please call me William." He said laughing.

"Oh, I can't my southern grandmother would not approve." Cara said in an exaggerated southern accent that made her sound like Scarlet from Gone with the Wind. She went into the house and as she did she flicked off the porch light.

Alison shook her head. "I have no idea who that girl was, but she was not my moody daughter."

William laughed, "She is a great kid."

"Well that great kid isn't usually that happy, polite and well behaved. I am not sure what happened to her." Alison said.

"I have that effect on women." William said jokingly. "Young and old they love me."

"Is that so?" Alison asked. She was stifling a laugh herself.

"Oh, yes" William said reaching for her, pulling her close to him. "I am a charmer and a true southern gentleman." He looked down at her face and smiled. Taking her chin in his hand he moved his mouth close to her lips so close that she felt the heat from him.

"I can make a woman weak in the knees with very little effort." William said. Alison closed her eyes waiting for him to kiss her. She had no doubt about his skills as her knees were quaking. He did not kiss her. He hovered just above her.

"Now, I will speak to you tomorrow. Go inside, take a nice hot shower, climb in bed and dream of me." With that, William turned, got in to the limo. Carl closed the door, got in the driver's seat and drove away.

Chapter Six

The café was jammed with people. Alison was scrambling to keep up with all the orders. She had four tables and one was seated with a family of eight. The menus, plates and coffee were flying. The manager, Fran called Alison over to the hostess podium by the door.

"You have to take one more table, ok Alison?" she said to the frazzled waitress.

"Seriously? Alison asked.

She looked over and saw William Porter in what had become is usual chair and table. "Ok, I will take Mr. Porter."

"No, Susan has him. You need to take table thirteen" the hostess said. Alison looked over across the dining room at table thirteen. She blanched when she saw who was sitting around it. Lance Gibson, his wife and son were sitting at the table looking at menus. Alison moaned. "No thanks."

"Well, you have no choice." Fran said. Alison sighed. She needed her job, so she sulked over to table thirteen where her lover and his wife sat. "Good morning, can I get you some coffee?" Alison asked not looking up from her ticket order pad where her pencil was hovering at the ready.

"Great" Mrs. Gibson said. "Your whore wants to know if we want coffee."

"Paula, really?" Lance whispered and then to Alison, "Yes, please coffee and what about you, Mikey, milk?" The boy looked up at his father with big brown eyes and nodded. Alison jotted it down and went to fetch the drinks.

"Do you really have to be so mean in public?" Lance asked his wife after Alison was gone.

"Truth is truth." Paula answered.

Lance and Paula Gibson had been married for almost sixteen years. Their marriage was not remarkable. They had the storybook life with a nice home complete with picket fence and a golden retriever. They had tried to have children early on. It was his idea. Paula tried to get him to wait. She didn't know why she had to be in a rush to have children. After years of trying, years of fertility doctors and ten years of failed attempts at invitro they had finally had a son. The stress of not getting pregnant almost did them in until the little boy had come in to their lives. The added stress of Lance's continual affair with Alison didn't help his wife's conception issues.

Lance and Alison had dated all through high school. He was set to marry her, bought a ring for her and planned to propose right after graduation. Everyone who knew them knew they would be the couple who made it work. The whole marrying your high school sweetheart thing and happily ever after was a

There and Back	Lori O'Gara

given for the high school power couple. The problem happened when Lance Gibson's father found out that Alison was from a middle-class family with a blue collar working father. Alison came from a long line of factory workers and Lance Gibson's family owned half of Georgia including the factories where her family members were employed. Alison's father, grandfather, and all her uncles had worked at nearby car parts assembly lines making bearings and gear boxes. She was not good enough for the Gibson heir. The old man told Lance if he married the girl he would not see a penny of the inheritance. Lance relented. He liked the lifestyle his family had given him and his sister. He had no desire to live in a lower tax bracket. That was it and the high school dream died. The problem was that the break was not clean. Alison was pregnant.

The Gibson family attempted to force Alison to have an abortion; however, she refused. Instead she hired a lawyer. After all was settled the agreement was clear. Alison received a check every month until the child was twenty-one and she was bound by a gag order. She was not allowed to speak the name of the baby's father to anyone including the baby, the child would not have the Gibson name and Lance would not be named on the birth certificate.

Alison was sent off to a home for pregnant girls so that she would be out of sight of the nosy Gibson public. It wasn't to protect Alison or for her wellbeing. It was solely to guard Mr. Gibson's son's precious reputation and by extension the reputation of the Gibson's profitable name. By the time that Cara Anne Elizabeth Lawson had come in to the world, Lance was engaged to his father's business partner's daughter.

When Cara was a child, like all children who have absent fathers do, she would ask about her father. When she asked about her daddy, Alison made up an elaborate story about a famous rock star who she had a one-night stand with that resulted in an accident baby. Cara liked the idea of being a rock star's kid and believed it. No one in town believed the story.

Everyone knew that Cara was a Gibson. Just about half the town owed money or their livelihood to the Gibson family. The entire town feared the power that the Gibsons wielded. No one ever breathed the truth about Cara in fear of retaliation or the dread of being driven out of town.

This arrangement worked well until Alison and Lance ran into each other at a New Year's Eve party three years after he had married Paula. The estranged lovers realized they still had a magnetic attraction to each other. They had sex in the laundry room of their mutual friend's house. The sex was hard, fast and dirty. Afterwards they agreed it could never happen again, but it did happen again. It happened several times over the years. Even when Paula found out just before she became pregnant with little Mikey Gibson, the ill-fated lovers did not stop meeting in secret. The last time was when Cara was fifteen, just a few short months ago. They once again promised not to see each other again.

They don't know exactly when or how Paula found out. She was hyped up on hormones one day and blurted it out that if Lance knocked up his whore again before he got his wife pregnant, she would take him to court for all she could get out of the Gibsons. Ultimately it was his guilt that kept him with his wife but not away from Alison. The threat of scandal or loss of money was not enough to keep Lance away from his addiction to Alison. He had to get his fix. She was his drug.

It took one more time of Lance telling Alison that he could not leave his wife for her to wake up. She finally realized that she deserved better than Lance Gibson. She had kept her resolve for seven months so far. The longest she has been out of Lance Gibson's bed since she was pregnant with Cara and Alison hated it. She hated the fact that he was with Paula. She missed him so bad some nights her body physically ached for him. Who ever said that time heals all wounds was a liar. If Alison could find the bastard she would show him a thing or two about pain.

Alison made her way to table thirteen with the coffee and milk. She walked past William and smiled. He nodded. She set the drinks in front of the family, took their breakfast order and went on with her work doing her best to ignore them. She treated them like any other customers in the restaurant.

Eventually they left, and the breakfast rush slowed down. Alison looked up and realized that William Porter was still at his table sipping on a glass of tomato juice. She went over and sat down across from him. "How is that non-bloody bloody mary?" she asked rubbing the back of her aching neck with her hand.

"Yea, I figured that I needed to stop drinking coffee after my fifth cup." William said with a wink.

"How on earth are you sitting still?" she asked. "I am not sitting still in my mind. I am doing a diligent job being your guardian." He said.

"My guardian?" Alison asked.

"I overheard what that woman said. If you could feel every dagger that she shot into your back every time you turned it in her direction you would need a stretcher to take you out of here." He said. "I thought you needed a bodyguard in case she decided to do what she was clearly plotting."

"Oh, I am not scared of Paula Gibson. She can't hurt me. If she does she will hurt herself." Alison said.

"I guess it would be bad for her if it got out that her husband is Cara's father." William said. Alison was in shock, "What? How do you know that? No one is supposed to know that"

"Alison, it doesn't take but one look at Cara and that man to know he is her father. The other thing, the way he looked at you spoke volumes. No wonder his wife wants you dead." He said. "Don't worry my sweet friend, your secret is safe with me, I promise. Does Cara know?"

"No and she can never know. William please, she can't." Alison pleaded.

"I said, you are safe with me. I am your self-appointed guardian." William said.

Alison felt a wave of warm relief wash over her. This man, this stranger promised her that she was safe. In her gut, she knew it was the truth. He reached over and stroked the top of her hand and her stomach was filled with fluttering. "Thank you." She managed to whisper.

William nodded. He did not know what this Gibson man had to hang over Alison, but he knew it was something that terrified her. He saw her face pale white as a crisp cotton bed sheet on his mother's clothes line blowing in Tennessee breeze. Alison's claim that she was not scared of the woman may be true, but she feared something. Maybe it was just Cara finding out about who her father was that upset Alison, but William thought it must go deeper than that. There was more than the worry over Cara that made Alison tremble in the presence of the coal colored haired man and his family.

William sighed. He rubbed his forehead. He knew before the thoughts formed clearly in his mind that he was supposed to be here to protect Alison Lawson, but why was a mystery.

Chapter Seven

The southern blue sky was clear, and the sun was high as Mark and Lauren walked through the square. The paths were scattered with mothers pushing babies in strollers and older couples walking hand in hand. Mark took Lauren's hand and smiled at her. They walked over to the large fountain in the middle of the square. The breeze kicked up the hem of Lauren's lavender dress and exposed her shapely legs that momentarily distracted Mark from his thoughts.

    Mark looked around Forsyth Park. He remembered reading somewhere that the park covers thirty acres just south of Gaston Street and north of Park Avenue. He saw the farmer's market and thought he would go over and buy

Lauren some flowers, but decided to keep his plan simple. "Come sit with me." He said to her leading her to an empty bench. She followed and sat.

"It is beautiful here." She said.

"So are you, you are beautiful." He said causing her to blush. A fine mist of water spray blew over them, but they did not notice. Lauren reached up and stroked Mark's face. He took a deep breath and began to speak. "I know we haven't know each other long, but I cannot see my life without you." He said.

Lauren's breath caught as she held the air in her lungs. She hung on his words waiting for what she was not ready to hear. Mark pulled a ring box out of his pocket. It was a bright aqua blue box with a gold calligraphy S on the top. Lauren recognized it as a ring box from Krystal Sabine, the famous jewelry designer from Perdido Key. Lauren's mind was racing as Mark moved and got on one knee. People who were walking by stopped and watched as he opened the box to reveal a large deep purple tanzanite stone set high on a white gold band. "Lauren Barton, will you do me the honor of becoming my wife?" Mark said.

    Lauren hesitated. Her heart screamed, "Say yes!" but her mind was speechless. The words did not accumulate in her mouth. She panicked. She wanted nothing more than to be Marks wife. She loved him with all her being. He was her perfect match, but if he knew her family's secret he would not have asked her. The worry clouded her face. Mark looked at her, his smile dropping. Lauren could not stand the sadness she saw beginning to fill his eyes. "Yes!" she shouted all at once and flung her arms around him. The moment swirled around them as applause erupted from onlookers. "a million times yes" she said. The dread of what she would have to eventually tell him left her as she kissed the man she knew was hers and hers alone.

Chapter Eight

Alison walked in to her childhood home and looked around. It was just as it had been for the past forty years. The furniture were all antiques, but they have been in this house her entire life. Her mother and father purchased the house soon after they were married. They had two boys. Just when they thought they were out of diapers, Alison showed up and surprised them all. She was a late in life accident baby. Her mother called her the oops blessing. There was just three years between Alison and her youngest brother. Her oldest brother was six years older. Both brothers now lived in Atlanta with their wives and children. Alison missed them as did their mother.

As usual her mother was sitting on the back porch enjoying her afternoon tea. Ever since her mother and father took a trip to England her mother had always considered herself honorary British and observed proper tea time without fail. When Elizabeth saw her daughter, her face lit up. "Come in my Darling and have tea with me." She said.

"Hi Mom." Alison dipped to hug her mother and kiss her on the cheek.

Elizabeth poured the tea and slid the sugar and cream over towards her daughter. Alison plopped two sugar cubes in her tea and a splash of cream. On second thought, she added one more cube. "How are you mom?" Alison asked and took a seat. Her mother sighed, and her eyes began to fill. "It's hard Allie. I miss your Daddy something awful and now the man from the bank is calling again. I don't know what to do." Elizabeth took her handkerchief and wiped the corners of her eyes.

"I know mom. I am doing all I can to find a solution. You will not lose this house." Alison said with determination.

"I hope so honey. I wish Bobby and John were here." Her mother smiled.

"Let's talk about something else." Alison said returning her mother's smile. "I met a nice man, a Christian man."

Elizabeth's head jerked up. "Really?"

Alison told her mom all about the enigma that is William Porter and about the evening they had spent together with Cara. "Wow that is amazing. Cara likes him?" Elizabeth asked.

"Yes, she even hugged him when she said goodnight." Alison confirmed.

"That is so not like her. He must be a very nice man" Alison's mom passed her a plate of small sandwiches made of cream cheese and cucumber. Alison popped one in her mouth and hummed with pleasure as she chewed.

"He is mom and he does something with real estate with his job. I am not sure exactly what it is he does other than negotiate deals with people who buy investment property. He said he can help with the house. I haven't told him all the details yet. I wanted to ask you first if it was ok to seek his help." Alison explained.

"Sure, honey I am willing to ask the pope for help at this point." Elizabeth said laughing. "God knows I am not even Catholic."

"Then it's settled. I will ask Mr. William Porter, the cowboy from Nashville Tennessee to help save your house." Alison decided.

"One more thing, if you want to win over this man, cook for him." Elizabeth instructed her daughter.

"Mom you know I am not that great of a cook. I am better waiting tables than filling them." Alison said worriedly. "I like this guy I do not what to scare him off."

"Listen dear, if there is one thing I know, I know men and their stomachs. If he has feelings for you in his heart he will eat whatever you set in front of him. If it is just business, he will pick at it like a crow picking corn off the ground." Elizabeth said.

Alison called Faith on her way home from her mother's house that afternoon. "Hey my friend, what's up?" Faith said picking up on the first ring.

"I need your help." Alison confessed. "What? Oh. My. The Alison Lawson needs my help?" Faith teased.

"Yeah, well I need to know how to cook for a man and flirt on a dinner date that I know will not end in sex." Alison said.

"I see why you called me and not one of your other friends." Alison could hear the smile in Faith's voice. "Come over to my house, now."

Faith's house was a penthouse apartment in the north historic district of downtown Savannah. Her Peyton Tower home was an open floor plan, with windows that went from the hardwood floor to the crown molding on the ceiling. Her kitchen would make any five-star restaurant chef envious. Alison made it to the elevator in record time and was sitting on a tweed sofa sucking down red wine in a matter of minutes.

"I don't know how to date a man who doesn't want to have sex with me." Alison said to Faith. Faith patted her friend's hand.

"It is easy. Cook and flirt. That is all. Then let him leave when he is ready to leave. Do all the things you normally do on a date, just leave your clothes on this time." Faith said in all seriousness without so much as a smile on her face. For some reason that made Alison laugh and as she knew spending time with Faith would do, Alison's anxiety left the building.

Faith broke out her favorite cookbook and the two women decided on a good honest southern dinner. Faith agreed with Alison's mother. "If he likes you he will eat whatever you set in front of him. If he hates it and tells you why it is bad, in a sweet way and tries not to hurt your feelings keep him. That will indicate he is comfortable enough with you not to play games and just be honest. That sort of gentleman is a rare find indeed." Alison wondered, in all her wisdom about men, why wasn't Faith married already. She asked Faith just that, "I haven't found the one God has for me yet."

"There you go with that God sending you a man garbage." Alison rolled her eyes.

"Alison, I believe it to be true and I will wait for that person. Why is it so hard to believe that a God who made the universe can't make a man for me or you for that matter?" Faith asked.

"I don't think he cares, that's all" Alison said.

"I pray and hope, Alison that God proves you wrong." Faith said. "I have to ask you a question though. I know you Allie. Why will this date not end in sex? I thought all your dates ended that way."

"I want to ask him to help with my mom's house and I really don't want it to appear that I am willing to sleep with him to get his help. You may not believe it, my friend, but I do have some morals." Both woman laughed.

They decided on a menu and Faith let Alison take her favorite cookbook with her when she left for home.

The next day Alison called William and invited him over to her house for dinner. Cara had an official movie date with Noah. After much begging and pleading from the teenagers Alison had agreed to let them go to a dark movie theater. This meant that Alison and William would be alone where she could tell him about her mother's house situation

Alison went through Faith's cookbook she had on loan and looked over the meal they had decided on, a simple but rich meal of fried chicken, fresh snapped green beans, whipped mashed potatoes, gravy and peach cobbler. She spent all afternoon preparing the meal and herself for the dinner with William. Is this a date, she asked herself. That remained to be seen, she thought.

After she had dinner prepared and cleaned her kitchen that looked like an explosion had happened in the pantry, she took a long shower and dressed in a teal bluish green dress. The hem fell just below her knees and the plunging neckline showed the top swell of her breasts. She painted her toenails and fingernails the same teal color. She decided to leave her hair down and flowing since most of the time William had seen her in the traditional waitress hairstyle of a swinging ponytail.

William knocked on her door at seven sharp. Alison deliberately let him knock twice before opening the door to see a smiling William with a single bright yellow rose in an extended hand.

"Lovely" she said.

"Yes, you are" William answered. He was taken aback at her color choice of dress. She was beautiful there was no doubt about that but the dress pained him with a memory of a Florida woman who was fond of a similar shade of blue.

Alison waved him in to the dining room where she had the table set for two. Against her better judgment she had lit candles around the room. William put his hat over on to the chair to his left as he sat down. Alison went into the kitchen and brought in a chilled bottle of red wine and two plates of salad. She sat a glass of ice tea next to William's plate and placing the salads on the table. She then poured herself a glass of wine. "Is sweet tea all right I remembered that you do not drink so I just thought…" Her voice trailed off. "Its fine. I am not picky." He said.

She sat down across from him and unfolded her napkin and placed in on her lap. William reached and grasped her hand. "Do you mind if I pray?" he asked her.

"Certainly not." She said and squeezed his hand. She bowed her head. William offered a prayer of thanks and they both said "Amen."

"This looks great, Alison" He said, "and something smells wonderful."

Alison smiled. "Call me Allie please. I hope you like good down home southern food." She said and blushed remembering what her mother had said to her about men and food.
"I do like good home cooking." He said. "It is a treat since I travel so much with my job, I don't get home cooked meals often at all." For a few minutes, they were quiet as they ate.

William noticed that Alison was fidgety. He felt the vibrations of her foot close to his shaking under the table. He wondered why she would be so anxious. She seemed to be a confident woman. Surely, she didn't have a reason to be nervous with him. Part of him was thrilled that his presence made her a bit on edge.

After they had finished their salads Alison brought in a plate full of fried chicken, a bowl of snap green beans, a bowl of mashed potatoes and gravy boat filled of a rich brown gravy. William let out a long whistle. "You weren't joking about the home cooking. This sort of meal would make my mother proud. She would have me married off to you based on no other information about you than this meal alone."

Alison beamed. "Well save room for desert. There is yummy goodness to follow." She teased. William filled his plate and ate without another word. He devoured three pieces of chicken and several spoonsful of the side dishes. After several minutes, he leaned back and stretched groaning. "This is the best fried chicken I have had in my entire life and I have eaten my fair share of chicken." William confessed. "I have to stop so I can see what amazing desert you have hidden away in that kitchen."

Alison laughed and went to the kitchen returning with a large pan full of peach cobbler and a container of vanilla ice cream. William melted as he took the first bite. He was in heaven and he told her so.

"That was the best food I have had in a long time. Thank you, Allie" William said to Alison as he licked the spoon of his last bite of cobbler. "I am so glad that you liked it. Let's go sit in the living room where we can chat a bit. Unless you are in a hurry to get home. It is getting late, but Cara won't be home for a while. She has a midnight curfew and she will walk in the door at twelve straight up." Alison said with a smile.

They sat down in the living room with satisfied bellies and warm hearts. They were content to sit and just be in the same room. They were silent for a long time. William draped his arm over the back of the sofa and laid his hand gently on Alison's shoulder caressing and stroking her skin just under the small cap sleeve of her dress. His fingers soothing her in to a peaceful state, so much so that she almost dozed off to sleep.

"You are beautiful." William said. Alison looked over at him to see that he was staring at her with a dreamy faraway look in his eyes.

"Well it isn't the wine talking for you, so I guess I must believe you." She said in a wistful voice that matched his expression. William kissed her firmly on the mouth. She returned his kiss. She let her mouth open to his. The sensation of floating came over her and she let it fill her body. She lost her thoughts to everything but this strong man who made her feel an awareness like no other before. She could not think of anything; her mind went blank even his name escaped her thoughts. There was nothing but the pleasure of his kiss and touch. When he finally pulled away from her she crash landed back in reality with an audible groan.

"Wow, I am so sorry for taking advantage of the situation. I should be going." He said shocking Alison.

"Wait, what?" she whispered. "You can't kiss me like that and just leave."

"Oh, I have to. I can't let this go any further." William said. "I want you Allie, God knows I do. However, I have a vow to keep."

"What vow?" Alison asked confused "Are you married? What vow?"

"No, sweet woman, I am not married." William sighed. "I made a promise to God that I would not have sex with another woman unless I made her my wife. I was in a bad situation that God got me through. It involved a woman who I was in love with. We were together for over a year. She ended up being a liar of the worst kind. I almost lost everything in my life. Thank God, I didn't. I will keep my vow to God for it. I am so sorry. I shouldn't have kissed you like that knowing I can't take it any further."

Alison mulled over what William had said. She weighed her words carefully, "William. I can respect the promise you made to God. I have not been completely honest with you."

William was surprised and said quickly. "You better explain yourself woman."

"I lured you here with food, candles and this sexy dress." Alison said pulling at the hem of her dress. "I did all this to ask you for help for my mother."

William relaxed, "Is that all? I swore to protect you and named myself your guardian. I will help your mother if I can." He let a small sideways smile play on his face. "That is not lying. That is using what resources you have to your advantage."

"If you say so. I was feeling rather guilty." Alison smiled coyly.

"Hush. Tell me about your mother." William insisted.

Alison told William how her father had given everything he had to his job. He lost time with his family to give them a fine home and a lifestyle that he thought they needed. As a result, he became sick with mesothelioma and died of lung cancer. A year before he died he had a stroke. Alison's mother spent the last year of her husband's life caring for him. The mortgage on their home got behind. The beautiful house that Mr. Lawson died for, that he worked so hard for his family to have, was at risk of foreclosure. Alison had no money to help her mother and her brothers refused to help. They wanted their mother to go live in a retirement home. The house was of no loss to them.

Alison had tears in her eyes, "My mother feels close to my dad in her house. I want her to stay there. I am afraid that if she has to leave it she will die too." Alison continued, "I was thinking since you do, well I don't know what you do exactly but since it has to do with real-estate I thought just maybe you could help my mom with some loophole." Her words came out in a rush of emotion

William smiled, "So, let me get this straight, you were going to seduce me Miss Lawson? You were going to use your womanly charm to woo me in to helping your mom."

"Don't put it that way, that makes me sound trashy." She said.

"You could never be trashy. It tells me you would do anything to help your mom. That makes you a good daughter." William said.

"Well it's no vow of celibacy, but I did make her a promise that I would do all I could to save her home." Alison said.

"A promise is a promise, Alison. A promise made to family is important. That is a noble thing you have done." William said. "I don't deal with that side of land deals. What I do is find property and broker it for rich clients who are wanting to buy land for investments."

Alison slumped, "So you can't help me."

"I didn't say that. I will make a few calls. You will need to give me all the information you have on your mother's home and mortgage company." William said.

Alison flung her arms around William's neck squeezing him tight. "Thank you, thank you!" He wrapped his arms around her too and pulled her close. "Don't thank me yet, it will cost you."

"Anything, you name it and I will do it." She said looking in to his eyes.

"You will have to fry chicken and make cobbler for me any time I ask for it from now until I take my last breath." William said. "I can't promise I can fix this for your mother but I will do everything in my power to stop it from happening,"

Alison pulled back and stuck out her right hand. "That is good enough for me. Let's shake on that deal." William laughed and shook her hand. Then he turned it over and kissed the back of it.

Chapter Nine

Cara looked behind her to make sure she wasn't being followed as she walked the almost deserted sidewalk. She didn't want anyone who might know her to see her and tell her mother where she was since she had no excuse to be on this side of town. She looked at the tall expensive townhomes that lined the street. She gazed at the number plates that were above the doors. Each one a different painted color and different style of number. Some were fancy with curls on the ends and others plain. None of them had the number Cara was looking for, two hundred seventy-eight. She was getting closer though as she just read two hundred and fifty-one. She wasn't sure what she would see when she found the correct building. She only knew that she had to find out what was going on.

Cara had been surprised to find the note stuck in her locker at school. It was typed. It simply read, "Do you want to know the truth?". It included a date and time for her to be at 278 West First Street. Cara was not a girl who acted on impulse, but she was a curious sort. The note was addressed to her so it must be safe to come here, she thought.

She looked up and saw the number she was searching for on a brownstone three story townhome. She walked up and rang the doorbell. She tapped her foot as she waited for someone to open the door. The door opened and an older man in a black suit stood there towering over Cara. He looked down at her and smiled a wiry thin line. "This way miss. The lady of the house is waiting for you." He said with a deliberate motion of his hand pointing with all his fingers in to the house. Cara walked into the foyer stopping in the center of the room under a glittering chandelier that filled the space of the fifteen-foot-high ceiling above her head. "This way" the giant man said.

Cara followed him through the house into a beautiful sitting room with plush white carpet and elegant furniture. The sofa was a soft sky blue. Cara was wondering if they felt as velvety as they looked just as the man motioned for her to sit down. She sat and stroked the arm of the sofa. It was downy soft under her finger tips. Across from the sofa were two matching blue chairs flanking a white marble fireplace that was almost as tall as Cara. Across the mantle were photos of people Cara had only seen on the television or occasionally on the sheets of her grandmother's newspaper. The Gibsons were local millionaires who owned half the city. "Hello Cara" said a silky deep woman's voice that made Cara spin around.

Standing in front of Cara was Paula Gibson in a pink summer dress and shoes the same hue. Her hands were weighted with heavy diamonds as were her neck and ears. The woman sat down in one of the chairs across from Cara. "I suppose you want to know why you are here." Paula said smoothly.

Cara picked at the fringe of her t-shirt. She felt extremely under dressed to be in this house with this fine lady. Don't say something stupid, she thought. "Yes mam." She said as sweetly as she could. She tried to stop picking she knew her mother would be mortified if she saw her doing it. "Cara, please call me Paula." The woman smiled. Cara's her face grew hot. She felt like what she imagined a lamb waiting for the lion to devour it would feel. She was terrified and did not know why.

"ok, Paula…" Cara said reluctantly. "What is the truth I need to know?"

"Have you ever wondered who your father is?" Paula asked in a purr.

Cara forced a smile, "Yes, but my mother told me some things about him."

"Oh?" Paula moved in her seat adjusting herself on the edge of the chair. "What sort of things did she tell you?"

"Well he was, is handsome. She said he is dark haired and I look like him." Cara said proudly.

"Yes, you do look like him Cara." Paula said.

It took a minute for it to sink inside Cara's conscience. She heard the words but did not comprehend at first what Paula Gibson had just said to her. When understanding hit Cara, it spread over her face. "What do you mean?" Cara whispered.

"I know your father and you look like him a great deal." Paula said and smiled. "Did you mother tell you his name?"

"No" Cara said timidly. "What is his name? Who is he?"

"I am not going to tell you unless you really want to know." Paula's voice oozed. "It is not something that you need to take lightly. You should consider how knowing his identity will affect your life Cara. You need to give it some consideration."

Cara's brow furrowed as she pondered the idea of her father. She had made up most of who she thought he was and his looks were all her imagination. Her mother had told her very little. Of course, she had to know. Then it hit her. If this woman knew who her father was, then her mother did too. Deep down Cara knew her mother's story about a rock star one-night stand was a lie. It just seemed too out of character for her mother to have slept with a stranger in one night of drunken passion.

"You shouldn't be the one to tell me. My mother should tell me." Cara reasoned.

"Ah but, why hasn't she? She has had your entire life to tell you the truth but she chose not to." Paula's words slithered off her lips. It occurred to Cara then that Paula Gibson had a point. Why had her mother not simply told her the truth about her father?

"Go home Cara. Think about what you want to know. Ask your mother if you would like and see what she says. If you do not get the answers you need, call me." She said as she stood and reached her hand out to Cara holding a bubble gum colored business card. Cara stood too and took the card.

"Ok, thank you Ms. Gibson, I mean Paula." Cara said.

Paula Gibson nodded. "James will drive you home." She led Cara out to the front foyer and opened the door. A man was standing next to a limo and opened the back door. Two limo rides in a month. What was the world coming to? Cara thought. This limo was plush and beautiful just like William Porter's rented one, but it was newer. Cara gave the driver her address and sat back. Her head was spinning. She could find out who her father is. She was scared and thrilled.

The car pulled up to the entrance of the mobile home park. Cara told the driver to let her out at the driveway. She did not know if her mother was home yet from the restaurant and she didn't want to explain her ride home. She said thank you and climbed out. She looked up at the drive towards her home and saw her mother in her jogging clothes standing there staring at her. Cara walked up slowly toward Alison who did not move. As she got close to her mother Cara smiled.

"Hi mom." She said lightly.

"Do not hi mom me, whose car was that?" Alison said.

"Oh, just a friend's no big mom. Relax." Cara knew when the words escaped her that she had said the worst thing possible to her mother at that moment. In a quick attempt to correct the mistake, she hugged her mom.

"Just a friend from school whose parents own a limo business. Maybe even the same one William uses." Cara said.

"William uses the hotel's car service." Alison said.

"Whatever mom. She offered me a ride and I took it. Two limo rides. I could get used to this." Cara laughed and walked away from Alison. Alison shook her head and smiled. Inside she cringed. She couldn't understand what was happening to Cara. She hugged me in broad daylight, Alison thought.

Cara went straight to her room, kicked off her shoes and turned on her stereo loud. Paula Gibson's words were circling above her. "I look like my father" Cara said out loud. Cara pulled out the chair to her desk and moved it in to her closet. She stood on the chair and reached up to the top shelf and dug around until she found it. It was difficult to pull out the large heavy book, but she managed without falling off the chair.

She opened the huge book across her bed and looked at the photos. It was full of photos of her mother as a child. The pictures where in chronological order up to the days just after Cara was born. Cara stared into the eyes of the young girl version of her mother holding the baby version of herself. Cara wondered if her mother was happy. She looked happy but there was something else in her eyes. Cara flipped over to the next page looking at more pictures of her newborn self and her mother. There was something there in the photos that drew Cara to them. Her mother's dark expression behind the smiles. Sadness? Exhaustion? She had just pushed a baby out to the world. There was something else there too. Then Cara saw it and recognized it. Determination, defiance and strength. Her mother, Alison Lawson looked like she was daring whoever was looking back at her to touch the baby. She was a mother lion protecting her cub. "What or who were you protecting me from?" Cara asked the teenage Alison in the photo. The picture Alison remained silent.

Chapter Ten

Lauren woke and left the bed. Mark was snoring loudly. She looked at her cell phone and saw three missed calls from her mother. She sighed. She didn't know how much longer she could keep her family's crazy drama from Mark. She was certain he would not tolerate it for long and she would lose him for sure. That was how it always worked out with men she had fallen for in her short adult life. They would find her attractive and amazing in bed. They would promise her the moon and stars. After they met her family they would all give her the same it's me not you excuse and run for the hills. She felt differently about Mark. She wanted to marry him. She saw a future with him. The prospect of him walking away petrified her. She knew she couldn't keep her family a secret for long, but until she figured out how to tell him she would keep it hidden. She looked at the elegant purple ring on her left hand and frowned. Maybe there was a way to keep Mark and deal with her family.

Mark stirred and she dropped her phone in to her bag. Slipping into the bed with him she snuggled down and wrapped her arms around him. His instinct caused him in his sleep to snake his arms around her pulling her face to his chest. Home, Lauren thought. This man is my home and I will not let go. She found herself saying out loud, "Don't let go" in a venerable voice. Mark moaned and replied in a sleepy tone, "Never."

Later, they were snapped out of the peace of sleep by the shrill ring of Lauren's forgotten cell phone. She jumped up and answered it. Mark wide awake sat up watching her. She answered and after a string of yeses and nods she discontented the call.

"I have to go back to Florida." She said to him with eyes full of regret. "It's my family."

Mark nodded as he began to prepare to leave Savannah. Picking up clothes out of the drawers and off hangers in the closet.

"Don't you want to know why?" she nervously asked Mark.

"No, my love. If you need to be with your family, then to your family I will take you." Mark said.

"Ok" Lauren said as she too packed her suitcase. Fear surged through her, but there was nothing she could do. She was headed to Florida to face her family with Mark by her side.

Chapter Eleven

William Porter stood in the doorway of the café waiting for Alison to get fished taking an order from an elderly couple. He was swaying back and forth with his hands in his pockets trying not to look conspicuous and agitated. He hated waiting. He looked at his Rolex and realized he was about fifteen minutes early. He motioned to the hostess. "I'm sorry. I have changed my mind I will take a table." He said. She led him to his usual spot and he ordered coffee. Alison smiled at him as she walked by. A few seconds later she walked up to his table, "I will be ready to go in less than ten minutes. Did you order food?" she asked.

"No, just coffee." William said. "Take your time."

"That's a good thing, my mother will want to feed us." Alison said with a smile.

Alison had planned for William to meet her mother. They were going to her parent's home to discuss the situation with the house. William did not make any promises, but he assured them he would try all he could to save Elizabeth Lawson's home. "If your mother cooks half as well as you do I am in big trouble." William said.

"Who do you think taught me how to cook?" Alison said with a laugh.

Just as Alison had predicted Elizabeth had cooked a large meal that consisted of fried pork chops, corn on the cob, potato salad, black eyed peas and hand cut biscuits. Around the hot food, the table was laden with plates of sliced fresh tomatoes, cucumber and cheese. In the middle of the table was a centerpiece that was a large pink frosted strawberry six-layer cake. There was enough food to feed a dozen people.

"Come in come in" chimed Elizabeth when Alison and William arrived. "Have a seat. What can I get y'all to drink?"

Alison and William said in unison, "Sweet iced tea." The trio laughed

"Sweet tea all around." Elizabeth said.

"This food looks amazing." William said, "Did you grow up eating this way all the time?"

"Yes, I did." Alison answered. "My mother cannot cook small."

Elizabeth stood at the head of the table and said grace. She then picked up the cake knife and cut three big pieces of the pink fluffy cake. She served it all around. William looked over at Alison confused.

"It's another tradition of this house." Alison said to William handing him a fork and pushed a plate of cake towards him. "Life is uncertain, eat dessert first."

"I have heard that saying before but have not seen it in action. I like this tradition." William said taking a big bite of cake followed by moans of pleasure. "Oh, my goodness. This cake is…. wow."

"Glad you like it." Elizabeth said giving Alison a knowing look.

"You southern women sure know how to treat a man." He said poking another bite in to his mouth.

"Well I am hoping that you will help me Mr. Porter." Elizabeth said.

"Tell me about your house. Ms. Lawson." William said through bites of strawberry heaven.

"I have to start at the beginning." she said. "Jack, that was my husband, Alison's father. He wanted to move here for a job in the factory. We were living in Fort Walton Beach Florida. It was a small fishing town back then not the big tourist place it is now."

"I know where that is. I did a land deal in Perdido Key a few years back." William said.

"Well if you didn't own a boat or have a trade finding a job was difficult. Jack was not good with his hands, bless his heart. He was also not good at construction and was seasick on the boats. He worked for his father for a bit but it was not paying the bills. When Alison came along we had to do something. My aunt lived here in Savannah. We came here so he could work at the canning factory. Peaches wouldn't you know." She laughed at the memory. "Eventually he got a job on the car parts assembly line. The pay was better."

"Here I was a born and raised Florida girl from the backwoods of Walton county in a big city like Savannah. I was scared to death. We lived with my aunt for several years and saved up to buy this house. It was smaller then. We added on the back sunroom and the den much later. Jack got promotions. After ten years of hard work and dedication he became foreman. We were in good shape financially. We raised our children here. Then Jack was diagnosed with cancer and had a stroke. He was not the same after. After two years of struggling to keep him alive and life the same, I was tired. Not just needing to sleep tired but the tired that never leaves your body and devourers your mind." She reached up and dabbed a napkin to the corner of her eye. "After Jack died I have done the best I could to keep this home, but the taxes and insurance go up every year. Then there are the medical and hospital bills that filled the mailbox. I am behind on the payments and the bank wants the house."

"How about some coffee William? Mom?" Alison asked. She needed to clear her mind. She knew the basics of what had happened to her mother, but she had never heard it all in one sitting explained by her mom. Alison went to the kitchen and poured water into the coffee maker. She looked in the cabinet where her mother kept the coffee. She reached in and grabbed the can of coffee. She looked again for the filters and did not see them. Maybe they are pushed back where I can't see them, she thought.

Alison grabbed a wooden step stool that sat in the corner. Smiling remembering how she sat on the stool watching her mom bake all sorts of goodies. To this day the smell of cinnamon reminds Alison of Sunday morning. She stepped up and reached in to the back of the dark cabinet. She found the filters and as she was pulling the package out her hand bumped a metal tin tea bag can. She dropped the filters on the counter and reached in pulling out the old can. It was rusty and looked ancient. Mom must have forgotten about it, Alison thought. As she pulled the can out she heard it clank. "Teabags do not clank," she said as she pried open the can, turned it over and watched a large brass key fall on to the counter. "The trunk key!" she said.

"What was that Honey?" Alison's mother asked from the dining room.

"Nothing. I found the filters." Alison quickly pulled her keys from her pocket and removed her mailbox key. She dropped in in the tin can and put the can back up in the cabinet.

Why hide the key mom, she thought as she slid the old key into her pocket.

William listened to Alison's mother tell her story. He did not see a sad widow with no money. He saw a true southern lady who loved her family and cherished her memories. He was wrong about Savannah. There was a damsel in distress to save and it was Elizabeth Lawson. He sucked in the breath taking several minutes of thought before he spoke.

"I can help you save your house Mrs. Lawson." William Porter said.

"If you do that Mr. Porter, call me Elizabeth." The old woman said with a nod.

"How?" Alison asked as she stepped back in to the dinning room.

"I have connections and I will do all I can using them. If that does not work I will give you the money to catch up the payments myself." He said.

"You can't do that." Alison said shaking her head.

"I can do whatever I damn well please with my money, Alison." He said with a smile but his voice was stern. The women both knew that this cowboy from Tennessee meant business, there was no doubt. Alison took her own napkin and smeared the tears that were streaming down her face.

Chapter Twelve

She didn't see the car. It was in the space behind her thoughts. The outside world was silent as she first walked then ran away from him. Her eyes clouded with unshed tears and her face wet with the ones that fell. Her mind knew it was over but her heart refused to believe it. She just wanted to get away fast as possible. She wanted to escape the disaster that was suffocating her. The words he spoke squeezing the life out of her love for him. When car struck her, she didn't feel it. In an instant, she was running then she was stopped flat on her back on the asphalt hot and smelling like gasoline. The crowd of people hovered over her. Disembodied faces of concern and terror.

She heard the call of the ambulance coming. Was someone hurt, she thought. She must get up and keep running. She didn't want to be here. She didn't want to know. She felt the ooze of something warm and wet. The scent of metallic blood mixed with the fumes from the car. She attempted to sit up but her head was heavy, bowling ball heavy. His words bounced around in her mind as she began to fade out of conscience.

"We can't see each other anymore. I have to marry her," he had said.

"But you love me." She had answered him. He had shaken his head and she had run.

The realization hit her perception as hard as the car had slammed into her body. Oh God, It's me. I am hurt. The baby, protect the baby her mind screamed.

Alison jolted up. She blinked at the dark room. The fog of sleep slowly lifting. She was in her bed sweating. A dream, a nightmare, she thought. A memory her heart whispered. Yes, but all had been fine after the accident. She was fine and Cara had been born perfect. God answered the prayer she couldn't vocalize on the pavement that day. She had been praying the same prayer ever since and so far, God had listened.

Alison climbed out of bed and padded softly down the hall to the room where Cara was sleeping. How many nights over the last sixteen years had Alison stood over Cara and watched the child sleep, thousands? Alison stood silent gently pushing a strand of Cara's hair off her face. Mother and child both at peace for a moment. Alison cherished these stolen seconds in which Cara was unaware of her mother's presence. The rebellious teen lost in the oblivion of slumber. She looked like a little girl still in love with ponies and cotton candy.

Alison hoped her daughter's dreams were sweet, not like the darkness that plagued her own. The stress of being the adult weighed heavy on Alison. Let someone carry a bit of it for you, came a voice in to her head. She sighed, if only she could, but who would do that for her? It is true she had financial help but she had no support. She held the weight of raising Cara solely on her own shoulders. She had no one she could depend on. Truth be told she would not trust anyone to help her. No one was ever good enough to be trusted with her jewel that was Cara.

A vivid image of William Porter flooded Alison's mind. He was standing in her living room hat in hand, his dark hair combed in a perfect Elvis Presley swirl, his smile soft and tempting. That man is handsome, she thought. Not let's raise kids together high school boy next door sort of cute, but let me take you to bed and have my way with you in a completely consenting adult way sort of beautiful. An ache began between her legs. A hot pulse that threatened to sway her balance as she made her way back to her own bed.

She collapsed across her mattress, reached for her cell phone on the nightstand. The clock on the screen blinks on and displayed three in the morning. She should call him. Then she remembered what he had told her and Cara. He made a promise to God. No sex outside of marriage. Alison groaned. She wanted what she always wanted, the impossible. The man who was not hers to hold and this time it was worse.

The man she wanted belonged to God not another woman. Can't compete with God, Alison thought. Well maybe she wouldn't have him but she could dream of him. Alison closed her eyes. She let the thoughts of William Porter touching her and kissing her fill her dozy brain. She wanted him, needed him to put his warm lips on hers. His strong hands too smooth to be a real cowboy's hands caressing her. She moaned as she drifted off back to sleep with images of the cowboy hovering over her that dark curl over one eye and adorable dimpled chin looking down at her.

Chapter Thirteen

Mark and Lauren were seated in the Chapin and Holster private leer waiting on the tarmac to take off. Lauren fidgeted and looked nervous. Mark had never seen her in this state. He reached over and gave her hand a squeeze. He waited for her to look over at him and when she did he smiled at her. She tried to smile but it did not reach her eyes. After the plane was in the air Mark braved asking Lauren how she was feeling. "I'm ok." Lauren said sighing heavily. "No, I am not ok"

"Would it help to tell me about your family. Why is seeing them so difficult for you" he asked. Lauren looked scared and paled. She didn't want to tell him her family secrets. She knew that keeping them from him would not do a lot of good. Mark, William too for that matter, is an expert detective even though they were not investigators. Lauren knew enough about what they managed to uncover while working on the Perdido Key land deal that convinced her that they could find out what closet her family kept the skeletons in with no trouble at all. She waved over the flight attendant and asked for a glass of red wine. "On second thought, go ahead and bring a bottle." Mark's eyebrow went up,

"Really?"

"Yes." She said.

The attendant poured her a glass of wine. She downed it in one gulp and motioned for the woman to pour another. It was after she downed the second glass and was waiting on a third that she spoke again. "I will tell you about my family Mark. I should warn you they, we are a crazy lot. I mean certifiable. I have a regular standing appointment with a shrink every other week. I have had this appointment for years."

"I see." Mark said "Lauren, I do not care what sort of mental issues you have. I love you for who you are and there is nothing you can do to change my mind."

Lauren felt his questions as he stared into her eyes. He did not know what the issues are and how he will have to deal with them. She knew it and it terrified her. She had no desire to tell him what to prepare for but she knew if they stood any chance in making an honest go at a real relationship, she must tell him.

"Well, I will tell you. My issues are because of my sister. She and I were very close. When we lived at home with our parents we were each other's anchor. She was, is damaged. I had to compensate for her deficits. My mother was in denial about my sister's condition for years. I see a shrink to help me deal with the residue of my family's influence on me, mostly my mother. I have come a long way. I finally know it was not my fault, but I still have things that I can't face."

Lauren looked over at Mark. She tried to gage how he was taking what she had admitted to. He was thoughtful. "I will be here with you, Lauren. I am not leaving you. You are the one for me and I will marry you." Mark said. "Now, that is all I need to know. We will deal with things as they come, together. Do you hear me Lauren? Together."

"Yes." She whispered and settled in for the reminder of the flight decided that it was not yet the time to tell Mark that her family heritage was greed and murder.

Chapter Fourteen

William sat on the balcony of his hotel room looking out across the river. The morning sun was just starting to color the sky in pinks, yellows and orange hues of watercolor clouds. He awoke in the middle of the morning with Alison Lawson's face in his mind. He did not know what had caused her to flash in his awareness strong enough to wake him. It wasn't just his mind that woke up. Other parts of his body wanted her. He had tried without success to ignore the feelings stirring in him. After tossing in the bed and fighting with himself to stop thinking about her he gave up. He showered, dressed and ordered breakfast. Thank God for room service, he thought as he slathered butter on toast and placed a fried egg on top of it.

As soon as his office in Nashville opened he planned to call his newest office associate to gather information about the bank that holds Elizabeth's mortgage. That woman trusted him with the only copy of her mortgage agreement. He was certain that he could find some sort of program that would help her. He had this nagging feeling that may not be the right answer.

After his call to the office William decided to go to the local branch of the South Georgia Bank armed with the Lawson's paperwork. The bank was an old typical southern red brick, white columned bigger than all the other structures around it city building. William walked in as if he owned the place. The lobby was full of people. There was a man standing at a tall marble topped table filling out a deposit slip. The elderly man counts his stack of bills repeatedly before his writes in the amount. William is surprised that in this age of mobile banking and internet banking that there would be so many people still doing their business the old-fashioned way with paper money and paper slips.

Over to the right were a group of desks manned with loan officers. At one desk was a very happy young couple who were just given the good news that they were approved for their first house. William couldn't help but smile with them. The husband wrapped his arms around his girl and hugged her close. Tears began to flow from them both. As William approached he realized the wife was very pregnant. First house and a baby, they are blessed, William thought.

A bank employee approached him and reached out his hand in Porter's direction. "Hello, what can I do for you sir?" the man in his mid-thirties said. "I am here for a client." William said as he pulled a blue folder he had been carrying under his arm.

"Certainly, right this way." The man motioned to a desk close by and walked around it. William sat as well.

"I am here about Ms. Elizabeth Lawson's mortgage account." William said.

"I will need her pass code and account number to help you mister, uh?" he said questioning.

"It's Porter, William Porter." William produces the account paper with Elizabeth's scrawling handwriting in the corner spelling out magnolia382 as the pass code. He also pulled out the power of attorney form. "I have everything you need right here. She has retained my firm to represent her in this matter and a few others." William said convincingly. The man looked over the papers that William handed him. William looked down at the nameplate on the desk.

"Listen Mr. Johnson, just tell me the balance of the account and the amount of the late payments. It is my intention to find a relief program for Ms. Lawson."

"I see." said Mr. Johnson clicking the keyboard on the computer on the desk. "the balance on the loan is fifty-two thousand seven hundred eighty-nine dollars and forty-five cents. She is behind three thousand twenty-four dollars and six cents. The next payment of one thousand and eight dollars will be due in a few days."

"Tell me about the hardship programs this institution has to offer my client." William said as he pulled himself up and glared at the banker. Mr. Johnson began to fumble around the desk and the drawers looking for something.

"The only program she qualifies for is this repayment plan that requires a modification of her loan. This may cause her interest rate to go up and her payback time to increase by a few years." He said laying a brochure on the desk in front of Porter. William looked at the terms of the program and did the math quickly in his head.

"Ms. Lawson must come up with over two thousand immediately. That will not work for her. She needs a better plan than that Mr. Johnson." William said.

"We have no other options for her at this point" The banker said.

The nagging feeling came back to William. Then a woman's voice came to him from off in a distance but clear as if someone was talking directly in to his ear. "You know what to do." William jerked his head around and saw no one even close to him. He was not sure where the voice came from. "Mr. Porter?" banker, Mr. Johnson asked him.

"Did you hear that?" William asked him.

"Hear what?" Johnson asked.

"Never mind." William said as he reached inside his jacket and pulled out his wallet. "I will pay the back payments and two more. That will give Ms. Lawson some time to get her finances adjusted, but Mr. Johnson. I want this done anonymously, do you understand?" Porter insisted.

"We are discrete here sir." Johnson said. William handed Mr. Johnson his platinum credit card. After the transaction had been completed, the two men stood. Johnson put his hand forward and William grasped it hard, shook the bankers hand strongly, nodded and walked out of the bank.

Chapter Fifteen

Paula Gibson was happy with how her plan was working thus far. She was certain that she would have Cara won over with just a few more conversations. If she could turn daughter against mother, then getting rid of Alison would be easy. Once Alison was gone from Savannah she would finally have her husband to herself. If befriending his bastard daughter was the only way to get him to stop this crazy obsession he had for the whore he had knocked up right out of high school, then so be it. Once Paula had dealt with the mother she would then dispose of Cara. A boarding school in Europe would do nicely. Lance would have to settle for having his child in a school someplace far away but Paula wouldn't have to see that doe eyed insult of a woman every time they went out in public. It seemed that everywhere they went there was some reason to see her or something that would inadvertently reminded Lance of her. Paula was tired of having the ghost of Lance's and Alison's love affair hanging over her marriage like a black cloud threatening to ruin every beautiful day with her husband and child.

Paula flipped through a book of sample fabrics. She was converting one of the guest rooms in to a room for Cara. She decided that a summer with Cara in the house would be enough to prove to Lance that she did indeed truly care about his daughter. She would spend the time as a devoted step mother then when the fall arrived she would convince him that the best thing they could do for Cara was give her the advantage of the best education that money could buy. Otherwise she would end up living the rest of her life in poverty as trailer trash she and her mother were. Paula would use her husband's pride and upbringing to her advantage.

The quiet room erupted in shouts as Mikey Gibson came stampeding through the house in to the sitting room where Paula was scheming. He held a toy jet plane in his hand making buzzing and swishing noises mimicking the sounds of a flying plane as he swooped the toy over his mother's head. "Attention flight 623 you are cleared for landing" the little boy said as he dove his plane on to the table spilling a cup of tea all over his mother's fabric samples and on to her lap.

"Mikey!" Paula shouted. "Where is that damn Nanny?"

"Dunno." Mikey said, "Sorry Mother" Just then a frazzled Nanny came in grabbing up the tea cup and attempted to clean up the mess from Paula's lap.

"Oh, stop it." Paula snapped. "Take him outside to play."

A phone started ringing in the other room and in a matter of seconds a young maid brought a cordless phone to Paula. "Hello, this is Paula" she answered.

Paula smiled. Yes, her plan is working nicely indeed, she thought.

Chapter Sixteen

The sun shone bright into Alison's kitchen as she twisted the mop over the sink. She has been up early after yet another dream filled with William Porter woke her. She had managed to scrub the bathtub, sweep the kitchen and mop every square inch of the floor. After which she cleaned out the refrigerator and sprayed cleaner in the oven. She did all the cleaning without waking Cara. Alison fished with the mop so she opened the back door and draped the mop over the rail of the porch. She heard a thud come from the other side of the house. She walked around the corner of the mobile home and saw Noah reaching up to kiss Cara who was leaning out of her bedroom window.

"Well, what is happening here?" Alison said. A shocked Cara said, "Nothing mother, Noah just stopped by for a minute."

"Umm Humm." Alison replied.

Noah said goodbye and left in a hurry. Cara closed her window and Alison went back into the kitchen. Cara walked in to the room the same time as her mother closed the back door.

"Cara, that is it. I am taking you to the doctor to get birth control. I cannot risk you getting pregnant." Alison said sternly.

"Mother, you don't understand. I am not having sex yet." Cara said.

"Yet. You will not see that boy again until we can do something about this foolishness." Alison decided.

"You can't stop me from seeing Noah. Mother!" Cara cried.

"I can, and I will." Alison said.

Cara stomped out of the room and slammed her bedroom door. Alison sighed. She wasn't sure how she was going to stop Cara from seeing Noah. Was it worth it anyway? She thought. She wanted to trust Cara she really did but the facts are teenagers will do whatever they want. All Alison could hope for was that she instilled the right sort of morals in to the kid when she was small.

Alison picked up the phone and called Cara's doctor. Alison was no taking any chances. Not with Cara's future. She was not going to allow her daughter to end up like she is now. Working two jobs just to keep a roof over her head and food in her stomach. Alison wanted better for her only child. Cara deserved the best in life and Alison was going to make sure that somehow her child would have better. Even if the ungrateful little shit did everything she could to make it difficult on her mother.

Cara sat on her bed flipping the pink business card between her fingers. Was her mother serious about Cara not seeing Noah? Cara did not know what the big deal was anyway, it wasn't like he had snuck in her window to have sex or even to sleep in her bed. Cara knew a lot of girls at school who were having sex with their boyfriends and other guys just for fun. Noah was not her boyfriend, not yet. He had not asked Cara to be his girlfriend, she hoped he would soon. Cara really liked him.

Cara wondered what her father would say about this situation. After all he got her mother pregnant when she was a teenager not much older than Cara was now. Maybe if she could meet him he would be more understanding about the situation than her mother. Alison was treating Cara like a child and she did not like it.

Cara looked at Paula Gibson's number. She picked up her cell phone and tapped in the number. Paula Gibson answered after the third ring.

"Hello, this is Paula." She said.

"Hi, it's…it's Cara."

"Hello dear, what can I do for you?" Paula Gibson's voice oozed imitation niceness through the phone.

"I want to know the truth." Cara said quickly before she changed her mind. "Who is my father?"

"Give me your address and I will send a car to fetch you." Paula said.

Thirty minutes later, Alison was in her room getting dressed when she heard a car pull up outside. She moved the curtain away for the window to see the same limo that had dropped Cara off parking in front of her home. The driver got out and walked around to the passenger side opening the door to the car just as Alison heard the front door slam.

Cara hurried out to the car with her backpack slung over her shoulder. She tossed it in and looked back at her mother's window. She did not smile or wave at Alison. The two stared at each other. Cara slid into the limo and the driver closed the door. As the car turned and pulled away from the driveway, Alison read the license plate, Gibson 1. Alison's knees buckled as she sank to the floor. A feeling of utter helplessness consumed her. I have lost her, Alison thought as sobs broke free from her.

 At the Gibson home, Cara waited on the same blue sofa as before. She tried to sit still and not panic. The butterflies in her stomach threatened to spill out every time she moved but sitting still was impossible. She stood and walked over to the mantle and looked at the family photos of the Gibson's family. Images of intimate family moments, vacations, weddings and such were scattered about in shiny silver frames. There wasn't any photographer posed photos with stiff poses, but the quality of the pictures told Cara that a professional photographer was the one who took most of them. They weren't fuzzy or off center like the hundreds of snapshots in her photo boxes at home that she and her mother had.

She picked up one that was of Paula and what appeared to be her husband on their wedding day. Paula was beaming and her husband was smiling a strained smile. His smile was just in his mouth it did not travel up to his eyes. Strange, Cara thought. He should be happy on his wedding day, right? He looked happy but not truly smiling. Cara's gaze dropped down the photo. Cara noticed that Paula had a tight grip on the man's hand. Tight enough his fingers looked slightly purple. "That was a great day" Paula said as she entered the room.

Cara quickly put the photo down. "I don't mean to pry. I was just looking." She said nervously.

"Oh, that's perfectly all right. Sit down child. I have asked my housekeeper to bring us some iced tea and snacks." Paula smiled a stiffly at Cara. Cara sat, Paula did not. Paula walked over to the mantel and picked up the photo that Cara was last looking at.

"Yes, a good day." Paula mused. "My husband, Lance Gibson is the heir to the Gibson fortune. Isn't he handsome? Some say that is the only reason I married him. Have you heard that viscous rumor Cara?"

"No mam. How long have you been married?" Cara asked.

"Two months before the day you were born." Paula said plainly.

Cara was shocked that Paula Gibson even knew when she was born. Paula turned to Cara. "Do you see anything familiar in this photo Cara?" Paula handed Cara a photo of Lance Gibson and two very pretty girls sitting on a stone wall with a beautiful garden surrounding them.

"No, should I?" Cara asked looking at the garden behind the three in the picture and then to the people. "I have seen them in the paper and on the news once or twice."

"Those girls Cara are your Aunt Holly and second cousin Casey." Paula revealed. "and Lance…"

Cara jumped up and stood before Paula Gibson "No don't say it. Please don't say it." Cara pleaded in a soft whisper and her body shaking. Paula smirked at Cara, "and Lance Gibson, my husband is your father Cara. You, my dear girl, are a Gibson."

Chapter Seventeen

William walked in to the diner and saw Alison immediately. Something was off. Her walk was slow and her shoulders where slumped. He went over and sat as his normal table. She made her way to him. He smiled up at her. "Sit." he said and she did not hesitate, she sat. "How are you?" He asked her. One look at her face told him something was terribly wrong. Her face was insipid, and she had purple circles under her eyes. She simply ducked her eyes from his and shook her head. "What is it Alison?" William's hand went to her cheek and lift her face to his.

"Cara" was all she managed to say before the big heavy tears dropped from her eyes landing in big splatters on the table between them.

"What about my favorite teenager?" William said trying to lighten her mood.

Alison explained that she had not seen Cara since yesterday and that she left in a Gibson's limo. "She had left in a huff, but I have a feeling she isn't at the Gibson's. She may have started out there but I bet she is at Noah's house. Noah won't answer his phone. I can't leave work. I can't afford to lose my job because my kid is being stupid. Otherwise I would go find Noah and ask him myself." She was visibly frustrated.

"Give me his address. I will go find out what he knows." William said. Relief flooded Alison's face.

"Thank you, William." She said as she scribbled down Noah's address passing it to William. William left his coffee on the table and walked out of the dinner. Climbing in to the car, he handed the driver the paper with Noah's address. Carl nodded, "Ah, money avenue. You have good taste in friends sir." Carl started the car and pulled it in to traffic.

As the car went across town William realized Noah lived within walking distance of Alison's and Cara's home, but the neighborhood was completely different. The car turned down a classic American dream street lined with tall trees and white picket fences in front of big red brick homes.

The limo stopped in front of one of the smaller but still elegant homes on the street. William jumped out not waiting for Carl to open the door. He strode straight to the front door and jabbed the doorbell. He listened and waited. After a few seconds, he banged on the door. A man with a scowled face wrenched the door open. "Can I help you?" he said.

"I am looking for Cara Lawson. She is a friend of Noah's and her mother needs her to come home."

The man interrupted William, "I know Cara and she isn't here. Noah is watching television alone."

"Could I please speak with him? Cara didn't come home last night and her mother is worried." William asked.

The man huffed "All right." He opened the door and let William walk into the house. "Wait here. I'll go get him."

William stood in the foyer and looked down the hall. He saw exactly why Cara liked Noah. His family was her ticket out of the trailer park. Well him or the Gibsons William thought.

"Hi" Noah said. "You're looking for Cara?"

"Yes, I am, err, a family friend" William answered.

"Well I promised her I wouldn't tell her mom where Cara went. She is safe, I can tell you that." Noah said.

Before William could think he grabbed Noah by the collar and pushed his back to the wall. "You will tell me where she is with details young man. I am not playing your teenager games. Capisce?"

Noah shook his head in shock and the cowboy who still had hold of him "Yes sir, she is at the Gibson's house. The big brown stone downtown."

"Thank you." William said smoothing the boy's shirt. "Stay in school Noah and while you're at it, keep your dick out of Cara and in your pants. If you take it out I know a guy who will take it off you." William turned and walked out of the house back to the car.

A short time later Alison and William were headed downtown. They both sat in silence. Alison was tapping her foot. When they reached the large brown stone on West first street Alison jumped out and slammed her fists on the door. "Open the damn door." She said. The door opened, and an older tall man opened the door.

"May I help you?" he said.

"Yes, this is Alison Lawson and we have reason to believe that her daughter Cara Lawson is here. We want to speak to her now." William said.

"This way sir and madam." Said the man motioning to them to come in to the house. Alison and William followed him to a sitting room with blue furniture. Neither one of them sat. Lance Gibson walked in to the room.

"Alison."

"Where is she Lance? Alison asked through clenched teeth.

"Alison, let's talk first." Lance said with pleading eyes as Paula Gibson walked up behind him.

"Lance, you know the conditions of our agreement. Leave us alone. Tell Cara to get herself in the car right now." Alison pushed past Lance and Paula backed away. Lance followed her lead.

Alison ran to the doorway shouting for Cara. Cara emerged at the top of the stairs. Cara looked strange in an expensive dress. Gone were her ripped jeans and black pink Floyd t-shirt she had showed up in the day before. Today Cara was wearing a knee length dress the same color as the sofa in the Gibson's sitting room.

"What is with crazy girls and the damn color blue?" William said under his breath. Alison looked over at him questioningly, "What are you talking about?"

"This girl I know, Krystal Sabine. That girl loves blue. Not just any blue but aqua ocean blue" He said looking at Alison's perplexed expression. "Forget it." Alison shook her head and turned back to Cara.

"Cara we are going home." Alison said.

"I don't want to mother." Cara said.

William walked past Alison and took the steps two and a time toward Cara. He leaned in a whispered into her ear. Cara's face fell and she nodded. "Ok, but I am not promising to stay away from here or the Gibsons mom. I will go with you now." Cara said.

Cara turned and went into a room to gather her things. Paula stepped up to William and Alison.

"She wants to stay, Alison. Why don't you just leave her here. You have had sixteen years to make a life with her. Give her father a chance to know her." Paula said.

"The agreement won't allow it and I would rather die first than leave my child here with you." Alison hissed.

"Actually" Paula pulled out a folded legal form "I have an order right here stating that she can stay if she so chooses. The terms of the original agreement still stand for you. Cara, however is not bound by it."

"How did she even find out about you Lance?" Alison said turning on her heel to face him. Lance shook his head.

"I told her." Paula's voice slithered from behind Alison. The small waitress stood toe to toe with Paula. "Stay away from my daughter. If you speak to her again, you will be sorry you ever knew my name." With that Cara, William and Alison left the Gibsons where they stood.

Within an hour later William, Alison and Cara sat in the living room of the Lawson mobile home. They were silent all but for an occasional deep brooding sigh that escaped Cara every few minutes. William cleared his throat as if to say something and Alison shot him a look which quickly changed his mind.

"How long are we going to sit here?" Cara said.

"However long it takes for me to not want to hurt you right now. What the hell were you thinking?" Alison said.

"I wanted to know the truth. You weren't telling me anything. You are treating me like a child."

"What truth did Paula and Lance Gibson tell you?" Alison asked certain that the secret of Cara's birth is not something they would have told her.

"They told me that you have been lying to me my entire life." Cara said defiantly. "Lance Gibson is my father."

Alison felt the air in the room leave her. She instantly deflated and put her head in to her hands. William reached over and put his hand on her back.

"Go ahead mother, deny it." Cara demanded.

"I can't." Alison whispered. "I was forced by the very people who betrayed that promise by telling you."

Alison raised her head and considered her daughter's eyes, the eyes of a Gibson full of tears.

William finally spoke. His voice deep and anchored in calm. "You both have been hurt. Now is the time when you must come together and be strong. There is bound to be some sort of fall out for this thing. Cara, your mother loves you. Everything she has done and said was for you."

Cara questioned. "and Mr. Porter, why did you say that to me on the stairs?"

"We are not talking about me Cara we are talking about your mother. She loves you. She has sacrificed a lot for you, suffered pain for you and you should be a little more grateful and respectful for what she has done for you." he said.

"Keeping me from my family, from my father?" Cara got up and stomped down the hallway to her bedroom and slammed the door.

Alison looks over at William eyes pleading filled with tears, "What am I going to do and what did you say to her?"

"I just asked her if it was the Gibsons she wanted to get to know or their money?" William said, "I also implied that Noah would not stick around long once she got wrapped up in the social calendar of the Gibsons. That her new family wouldn't be as tolerant as you are with the boy climbing out the window and maybe she should think about it for a little bit if she truly loved him. I played on the infatuation that all teenage girls have with the bad boy in school."

"You took a gamble." Alison said.

"Yea I gambled and hit a small payout. At least I distracted her enough to get her to come home."

William stopped suddenly and grabbed Alison by the shoulders. "I have an idea." William said quickly. "Pack a suitcase. Tell Cara to pack. You won't need much we can buy stuff when we get there."

"Wait, what? Pack? William?" Alison was confused. "What the hell are you talking about?"

"You two need to get as far away as you can from the Gibsons and fast." William said.

"What are you saying?" Alison asked confused. "I am not wealthy like you William, I have a job. I can't just leave. How long will we be gone? There is my mother and her house and…"

"Alison" William placed his hands on her face. "It's ok. Call Fran and the parts store manager. Tell them you need a week or two off. Family emergency and all that. Leave the rest to me. You must do this Alison." William bent down and kissed her lightly on the lips, got up and left without another word.

Chapter Eighteen

The next day Cara staring out the window in English class lost in thought about the Gibson's and her mother. She was sort of proud that her mother acted like a momma bear protecting her cub. The class bell rang shocking her from her thoughts. She walked out to the hall and down to her locker. She turned the dial left then right stopping at the correct numbers. She opened it and saw in the reflection of the mirror on the door the smiling face of Noah that made her jump.

"Gee whizz Noah you scared the shit out of me." Cara said.

"Sorry babe, hey so what's this I hear about your mother confronting the Gibsons?" he asked her. "And don't be mad. That man came to my house and threatened me. I had to tell him where you were."

"Ugh, can no one keep a secret around here but my mother?" Cara said.

Cara told Noah what happened as they walked out to his car. She went to the passenger's side and Noah opened the door for her. She smiled, kissed him quickly and climbed in the car. Noah got in to the driver's seat. "Your mom, Cara, is bad ass" he said. "Makes me want to cancel the plans I have for us this afternoon."

"Oh, no you don't Noah James. You promised me an afternoon I would never forget." Cara said with a sly smile. "Now what have you planned?"

Noah smiled, "Wait. First, what did you tell your mom about tonight?"

"I am having a sleepover at Jane's house. She will cover for me if my mother calls there and I have my cell see?" Cara said holding up her phone. "Mom wasn't happy about it but she let me go anyway." Cara shrugged.

"Just as long as you were convincing. I don't want to be on the wrong side of your mother." They both laughed but somehow Cara thought Noah meant it.

Noah steered his car on to highway eighty towards Tybee Island turning the radio up. He knew Cara would sing if he did. Cara belted out with the song on the radio. He drove until he pulled up at a campground on the island. He turned off the car in front of a large blue tent. Cara looked over at him.

"We are staying here tonight?" she asked.

"Yes. Listen no pressure ok? We don't have to do anything but hold each other all night if that is what you want. I don't want to force you into doing something you are not ready for."

"Ok" Cara said. Her stomach was a twist of knots and turmoil. She knew that boys said all the right things to girls in the hopes of getting laid. She was no fool and she was not ready for sex, that she knew for sure. She loved Noah and didn't want to lose his friendship.

They decided to take a walk to find firewood. Noah had thought of everything. He brought hotdogs on skewers, chips and soda. He even included all the ingredients to make s'mores. Cara was surprised that Noah knew how to make a campfire. It took a little bit of work to get it to start but he manipulated the matches and a pile of dry leaves to get the fire going. He added pine cones and the flames grew quickly. They enjoyed a dinner cooked up over the campfire and soda that Noah had in an ice chest.

Cara noticed some wine coolers and a half gallon of milk down in the ice. When she asked Noah about the milk he reached into the tent and pulled out a box of bright sugar-coated cereal with a crazy looking bird on the front.

"Breakfast" he said with a boyish grin.

After they finished eating, Noah found two long sticks that he fashioned to sharp points on the ends with his pocket knife sliding two marshmallows on to each of the pointy ends. Cara watched him curiously. He looked over and saw her puzzled expression. "Trust me, for an authentic s'more you need to use a tree stick." Noah explained it isn't the same with a metal skewer."

Cara held her marshmallows over the flames until they were perfectly brown and then she squished them between two graham crackers with a square of chocolate bar. She hummed with pleasure as she took a bite and licked the chocolate that ran down her fingers. Noah sat mesmerized at the sight of Cara enjoying the s'more like a little girl. "Umm, yeah see what you mean" she said to Noah.

After she had finished she excused herself to the bathrooms to take a shower. When she returned, she saw that Noah has also managed a shower. He handed her a wine cooler and they sat down looking at the fire. Cara's mind was racing, she was still trying to get her head around her mother's lies and now she feared disappointing Noah. Yes, he said he didn't want to pressure her but he had gone through so much trouble to make the night nice. She felt like he expected something to happen.

Noah yawned, "Ready to go to sleep?"

"Yes, but Noah…"

"Cara it's ok. Just let me hold you while we sleep. That is enough for me. Just being with you is all I want. I love you, Cara." Noah said and extended his hand to her. Cara took his hand and followed him into the tent.

Chapter Nineteen

Alison did as William instructed. She called Fran who was not happy but agreed to her having two weeks off. The parts manager was easier to convince as Alison worked part time there anyway. Alison had no idea where they were going so she packed as she would for a road trip. Cara came in to the house closing the door softly behind her.

"How was your night with Jane?" Alison asked startling Cara.

Cara stammered, "F…Fine. Why?"

"Just asking. Sit I have something to tell you." Alison explained that they are going to go on vacation with William Porter. Before Cara could object Alison told her to pack her bags. Cara did so but complained the entire time about how unfair her mother was for taking her away from her new family and friends. Then Cara proceeded to have a ten-minute monolog about how ridiculous it was to go off on a trip with William, who they barely knew, to God knew where to do heaven knows what. Alison was amazed that Cara, her openly anti-religious daughter referenced God and heaven in the same rant; however, she did not respond to her daughter's outburst.

    Despite the headache that Cara gave her Alison was looking forward to whatever adventure William had planned. Just the idea of being out of town where she would not run in Lance or Paula thrilled Alison. William told her that the plan was for her and Cara to reconnect some place where the Gibson's would not be there to distract Cara with their spin on the truth and their version of reality. This would give Alison time to tell Cara the truth and show her daughter how much she loved her. Two days later the three of them were on Chapin and Holster's private leer headed south.

They landed at Pensacola International Airport where a limo was waiting on the tarmac. When the cowboy and the two ladies departed from the plane, the sun was blinding and hot. Alison and Cara still had no clue where exactly they were because William gave the crew direct orders not to announce the destination over the intercom on the plane.

"Where are we?" Cara asked as the car left the airport.

"You'll see." William said. Cara reached for her cell phone and William quickly took it from her hand.

"Hey." She objected.

"No phones." William said and took his phone out of his pocket and turned it off. Cara and William looked over at Alison who tried to ignore both.

"What?" she said looking innocent.

"Hand it over." Cara demanded.

Alison sighed and handed William her phone too. He opened his briefcase that was on the floor next to his feet and put all three of the phones in the case and locked it. He looked up and smiled.

Cara was looking out the window and Alison was looking out the opposite window. Both women looked like little girls pouting about not getting what they wanted for Christmas. William stifled a snicker. "Oh, my goodness, cheer up you two. I promise this will be a grand adventure." William said bursting into laughter.

The car weaved and meandered through downtown Pensacola. On several intersections corners, there where statues of pelicans painted in wild colors and themes. "What's with the pelicans?" Cara asked. William explained very careful not to give away the name if the city that Pelicans in Paradise was a public art project organized by the local newspaper in which pelican statues made from fiberglass are decorated by various artists, selected by sponsors, and placed at various outdoor locations around the downtown part of the city. Pelicans in Paradise was inspired by the similar Cow Parade project in Portland, Oregon. Each fiberglass pelican was nearly five feet tall and weighed about seventy pounds. A total of forty-one pelicans have been specially made for the project depicting art ranging from a dollar bill, abstract shapes, flags and military honors.

"I think they are cool." The teenager said and almost smiled.

The driver kept going past the city limits on to a straight two-lane highway. Tall pine trees lined the edges of the roadway as the buildings faded off behind them. William reached over and let down both windows in the doors of the limo and slid open the sunroof. The sun was shining and the breeze flooded in filling the space with fresh clean air. They all took a deep breath. Cara closed her eyes breathing deeply several times.

"What is that amazing smell?" Cara asked.

"It smells like…. sweet salt?" Alison said. William laughed, "Close. You'll see. We are almost there."

The car rounded a corner and began to ascend a large hill. William told both girls to look out the window. What they saw thrilled them. They saw that the hill was the large swell of a very tall bridge over what looked like a river. The car began to descend the opposite side of the bridge and that is when they saw where the smell was coming from and Cara squealed. "Is that the ocean?" She exclaimed.

"Well sort of, it is a Gulf, the Gulf of Mexico." William said.

Alison grabbed his arm. Her face was beaming, "William, Florida? You took us to Florida?" William smiled as the two women watched the coast of Perdido Key go past the windows of the car.

The car finally stopped outside a tall resort building and a door man opened the door for them to exit. Cara was dumbfounded and could not speak. This did not go unnoticed to Alison and William who exchanged knowing glances.

"Hello Mr. Porter." The man said, "How was your flight?"

"It was great. Thank you for asking."

As they walked through the doors in to the lobby the two women were filled with a sense of awe. The room was lit with a huge crystal chandelier. There were elegant sitting areas and calypso music filled the air. The back wall of the lobby was spanned with a tall black marble service desk. When they approached, the woman behind the desk spoke to William.

"Hello Mr. Porter we have the penthouse suites ready for you as requested."

"Good." William said taking the key card from the woman's hand. "and Carlos?"

"Yes, he is on his way down now." The woman said. Then turning to Alison and Cara the woman said, "Welcome to Eden."

"The penthouse? Eden?" Alison said.

"Sure, it has three bedrooms. That way you and Cara have your privacy and it feels more like an apartment not a hotel room." William said.

"Why are you doing this for us, William?" Alison asked feeling extremely overwhelmed.

"Because you two are important to me." William said.

The group entered the elevator that moved swiftly up. A few minutes later the door chimed. They got off the elevator and walked to the door. The numbers, 512 glistened on a brass plate in the dim light of the hallway. William slid the card key through the readers and opened the door for the women to walk through. Behind them he heard solid footsteps approaching. William turned around to see his favorite porter pushing the luggage cart with their few bags. A tall dark complected man came striding toward William. His smiled filled his face as he reached his hand out to shake William's vigorously. "Mr. Porter, so nice to see you again. We have the rooms ready."

"Carlos my friend! How's the family?" William said forcefully shaking the man's hand.

"Oh, fine fine Mr. Porter. Glad to see you." Carlos said and smiled at Alison. "Let me get your bags in sir. Must not keep your lady waiting. I am Carlos." He said, and he took Alison's hand and kissed the back of it softly. "Whatever you need Ms. Lawson, Carlos will provide"

"Thank you." Alison said as Carlos greeted Cara. He then turned and said, "Follow Carlos."

Alison whispered to William. "How did he know my name?"

William smiled, "Because I told him, and he will not forget it once he has heard it."

"Look at this bathroom!" shouted Cara from somewhere deep in the penthouse. Alison was amazed at the grand scale of the rooms. The ceilings were high and the panels on the wall were a dark wood that had a reddish glow to the mirror like shine. She meandered her way around the furniture looked like fine antiques that would be at home in any gallery in Savannah. She slipped her shoes off her feet and dug her toes in the plush dark green carpet and padded her way down a hallway in the direction of Cara's laughter and "oh my God, look at this." The teen exclaimed.

Alison found her sitting fully clothed in a large bathtub that appeared to be made of copper. The floor was a cool marble under Alison's feet. She took in the space and walked through the opposite door in to a huge bedroom with a four posted bed that looked like it should be in Cinderella's castle draped with a rich purple brocade fabric. Carlos walked past her placing her bags on a bench that was close to a full walk in closet.

"Here you go miss. A suite maid will be in later to unpack for you so don't bother yourself with all that. If you need anything call 811 and Carlos will be right here for you, day or night." Carlos said patting his chest with his fist, turning on his heel and leaving the room.

That's enough, Alison thought and strode back through the hallway to find William Porter. She had to find out just what William was after. Why would a man she barely knew take her and her troublesome daughter to a place like this, this paradise? He had to want something, something from her or maybe Cara. She was hot to find out what his deal was, and she had to find out fast. She was certain that she could trust him but it was all just too much. Too much money, too much unbelievable and too much perfect. He was perfect. He was the most unselfish man she had ever met. From her experience men were not unselfish. They always wanted something from women, in return for every small nice thing they did and what William was doing was not small at all.

She found William standing on the balcony looking over the beautiful waves that crashed onto the sugar white sand beaches of the gulf. He pointed off in the distance without saying a word, Alison's gaze followed his fingers and she saw a pod of dolphins rolling in the waves. One jumped in a spiral and splashed back down into the water. It was like nothing she had seen before. She had seen dolphins on television but never in the water. Hell, she had never seen the ocean before today. The bottle nosed swimmers looked like there were right off shore. She started at them in amazement captivated by their grace and beauty. She continued to watch them until they drifted off into the distance and she could no longer see the gray bumps going up and down in the waves.

She realized that the anxiety she had felt a few minutes before, the stress that she was going to ask William to explain his intentions had completely left her. She meant to question him as to why he would bring her and Cara to such a beautiful place. The need to ask him disappeared as she took in a deep breath of the clean salt air.

William stood next to her, his eyes closed, simply breathing. He has missed this place. He glanced over at Alison who was staring at the water.

"Amazing isn't it? He said.

"Yes." Came her breathy replay.

"Look I know you want to know why I decided to bring you and Cara here. This place is magical. It has a healing power that I can't explain other than it comes from God." William looked in to her eyes as a look of shock changed her expression.

"I...I can't. How did you know that I came out here to find you to ask you that very question?" she said.

"What question?"

"Why did you bring us here." She said.

"I just knew you wanted to know. I felt the question come from you as you walked out here. I heard it in my" he paused looking for the right word, "in my heart. There is magic here, Alison. Listen to me, I am telling you if the magic that is here can't fix you and Cara nothing can. I have seen it work miracles and I felt it for myself."

"Look William I can't begin to thank you enough for all you have done for me and Cara. For helping my mother with her house, but I do not believe in such stuff as magic. It is fantasy, fairytale little kid stuff. I can't deny it is beautiful here, but magic? Really? You a clever businessman and devoted Christian who does not believe fantasy magic, do you William?" Alison said skeptically.

"Alison" he said taking her hands in his "Yes I do. I have seen it with my own eyes. Give it some time, you will see it too." William said pleading.

Cara came bouncing out onto the balcony. "What are you two talking about? You look so serious." She said grinning, "This place is crazy cool Mr. Porter."

"Please sweet girl stop calling my Mr. Porter or I won't tell you the surprise I have for you for tomorrow. It is William from now on, got it?" he said laughing and Cara nodded.

"Mom, I could live here. Let's move here." She said. Alison just shook her head and went to find the copper plated bathroom. Was the toilet copper too? Either way she didn't care what the privy was plated with, magic or not.

Chapter Twenty

Alison made her way to the kitchen surprised to find the coffee pot full. There were platters of fruit, bagels and other a continental style breakfast items waiting on the counter. She poured herself a cup and went out on the balcony. She sat down and looked out across the water. The sun was bright and the white sand gleamed like powdered glass. Off in the distance there were people walking along the shoreline occasionally stopping to pick up what Alison assumed were seashells. She watched as the tourists came and went when she finally recognized a couple coming closer. William and Cara were walking side by side laughing and talking. Of course, Alison was too far up to hear what they were saying. After a bit, the pair came up to the penthouse joining her on the balcony sitting across the table helping themselves to breakfast. "Look mom." Cara said placing a handful of shells on the table. There were pink, orange, white and glittering ones.

"Beautiful" Alison said. "How early did you two get up this morning?"

"Oh, I was up at daylight. I was too excited to sleep in." Cara said slathering cream cheese on a bagel.

William sat down sipping coffee. "So ladies are you ready for an adventure?"

"Yes" Cara answered. "but I can't imagine it getting any better than walking on the beach. Mom, you have to go walk out there. Your feet make this crazy squeaking sound on the sand. The water is warm and feels amazing."

Alison smiled at her daughter. "Who are you and what have you done with my child?" There was a knock on the door.

William looked over at Alison, "Why don't you go answer that."

Alison went to the door and opened it to find her friend Faith standing in the hall way. The two women squealed in excitement. "How? What are you doing here?" Alison said as she threw her arms around her friend.

"William invited me." Faith said simply. "Get dressed. We are going shopping"

Alison looked over at William who nodded. Without a second thought Alison ran to him and wrapped her arms around his neck. She pulled him into her and kissed him hard on the lips. His mouth opened to hers and they kissed for several minutes before they breathlessly pulled apart. "Thank you" she whispered into his neck.

"You are very welcome. I figured you could use a friend right now." He said. "Please have a good time and charge anything you want to the room. If I hear of you seeing something and putting it down because of cost I will not be happy. Put your pride away and do this for me." Alison nodded. "ok, William."

William called a car to take Faith and Alison to a shopping court not far from the resort. The buildings were bright candy colored with delicate white gingerbread work. The women walked from store to store chatting and laughing. Alison found a couple of pretty sundresses in a clothing boutique. Then of course "you will need new shoes to wear with the dresses." Faith had said. Alison found a strappy silver pair of sandals and a red pair of three inch heeled pumps. Then they went to a store that sold more formal style gowns. Faith took Alison by the hand and pulled her inside. They tried on several cocktail dresses. Alison looked especially good in a knee length green dress. Admiring her figure in a mirror she decided to buy it. "You look amazing." Faith said. "What is different about you?"

"Stress. I look tired." Alison said with a chuckle.

"Listen, you need some dangling earrings." Faith said. "I saw a jewelry store close by the entrance."

The two women walked up to a jewelry store that was all glass and blue. They opened the door and were confronted with soft blue carpet under their feet, sounds of calypso music and the smell of coconut. The walls were lined with sparkling glass cases full of all sorts of glittering bobbles of gold, silver, diamonds and a rainbow of gemstones. Faith sucked in her breathe as she looked around.

"This is a beautiful store." She said and Alison agreed. They looked at all the cases slowly taking in the unique styles and colors. There was a case full of flawless, unblemished pearls set in gold. In the next glass box were individual rings with stones ranging from the deepest cobalt to the lightest lime green. They eventually made it to the boxed glass case with the earrings. There were hoops, studs and long strands of silver and gold. A sales woman approached them.

"Hello, how can I help you?" she said with a slight Italian accent.

"My friend needs some chandler earrings." Faith said. "She bought this awesome dress and she needs them to finish off the outfit. I am thinking sliver."

The woman pulled out a tray of earrings. After careful consideration, Alison decided on two pairs of earrings. The sales woman wrapped them in blue paper and then put them in a white box tied with a blue ribbon. "How will you be purchasing these today?"

Alison pulls out the card that William gave her and hands it to the woman. The woman looks at it strangely but runs it through the credit card reader just the same. "Excuse me a minute." She said and walks through a door to a back office.

"I'm sure it was approved. What is she doing?" faith said annoyed.

The woman came back to where Alison and Faith were waiting. Behind her walked a slender woman with long coppery brown hair in a blue dress the same aqua blue as the rest of the room. Alison thought the woman looked familiar then she realized it was the dress. It was eerily similarly to the one Cara had on when Alison went to get her from the Gibson's house.

"Hi, my name is Krystal Sabine. Eva tells me you are using William Porter's business card. Is he with you?" Krystal asked.

"No, he told us to use it." Faith said, but Krystal was looking at Alison. "Well it just so happens that he is a dear friend of mine and it is not like him to give a pretty woman is credit card." Krystal insisted.

"It's ok, I understand, but if he is your friend please call him and verify that I can use his card. My name is Alison Lawson." She said.

Krystal looked at her and smiled. "Sure, I will do that." After a few seconds, Krystal emerged. "I apologize. I had to be sure."

Alison smiled back but coolly answered. "Like I said, I understand."

"Let me make it up to you. You and William will come to my house for dinner. I would love to catch up with him and get to know you. Bring your friend and daughter too of course. How's tomorrow?"

"That's kind of you. I will see if William wants too." Alison said cautiously.

"Nonsense I will call him back and tell him to come. He knows my address well." Krystal said not taking no for an answer.

"I just don't know. I should really check with William." Alison stammered.

"Come with me." Krystal said as she grabbed Alison's hand and lead her to a back office. Faith followed. Krystal pulled out her cell, showed Alison the screen that had a photo of a smiling William and his number displayed under his face. The woman touched the call icon and the phone dialed a number.

Alison only heard one side of the conversation and it was mainly yessing and I sees that came from the pretty woman in the blue dress. Suddenly the woman clicked the speaker icon and William's voice came out loud and clear. "ok, we will come for dinner."

"Thank you, William." Krystal said and disconnected the call.

"Well, we will see you then. Can I bring anything?" Alison asked the stranger.

"No no, just you and your people." Krystal said.

Faith looked from the woman in the blue dress to her friend and back to the woman. What just happened, she thought.

After she and Alison left the store she said those very thoughts to her friend.

"I have no idea what happened." Alison said. "She said she is a good friend of William's so I guess it is all right to go have dinner. You don't have to if you don't want to."

"Good friend? More like an ex-girlfriend. I know a jealous ex when I see one." Faith said. Alison thought about the woman and the comment William had made about blue when he had seen Cara in a similar dress. Then she remembered that he did mention Krystal's name. "Maybe she is the girlfriend, but I saw a large blue ring and a wide silver wedding band on her finger too. She is a married woman or at least portrays herself as married. Besides he is certainly attracted to me." Alison said and blushed.

"How do you know that?" Faith asked.

"He has kissed me and called me beautiful a few times." Alison confessed.

"Really?" Faith said, "Do tell?"

"Stop it, there is nothing to tell." Alison said. "He has a commitment to God. He is more your type than mine for sure. He is one of your good Christian men. No sex before marriage and all that. I do not have room in my life for that sort of Mr. Morality."

"It might do you some good to make room in your life for that kind of man, Alison." Faith said. "Stop trying to blow off your relationship as nothing. I saw you too together. He flew us to Florida."

"I would rather take that sexy cowboy to my bed and do some not so Christian things to him." Alison said with a giggle.

"You better get on your knees and pray for forgiveness Alison Lawson. You are so naughty" Faith said.

"Yeah but it would be oh so much more fun being naughty with William Porter." Alison said.

Chapter Twenty One

"Cara, since your mother and Faith are off doing that retail therapy that girls like to do, you are with me today. Is that ok?" William said.

"Sure, where are we going?" Cara asked.

"We will see. I have a shop I need to stop at that sells the best wine and cheese on the key." He answered.

"You could ask mom to pick it up and we could go swimming instead." She said.

"I could and then we wouldn't have time for the best part. I have something magical to show you." He grinned. "Get yourself ready to go."

William went into the room where he was staying. He pulled out a blue shirt and white shorts. He wanted to be prepared in case he ran into any of his friends on the key. He wanted to look the part of resident not a tourist. Even though he wasn't a true resident he still felt like he was part of the small group of locals that he called his friends and some he even referred to as family. He showered and dressed quickly.

When he walked out into the living room Cara was searching fanatically all over the place. She looked under the sofa cushions, on top of tables, and under chairs. She was in a hunt for something but William couldn't not discern what it was that she had lost.

"What are you looking for Cara?" he finally asked.

"My Tardis." She said.

"Your what?" he asked.

"You don't know what a Tardis is?" William shook his head.

"You have traveled around the world and have never meet a Whovian?" Cara asked amused. "I will give you a hint, it is bigger on the inside than it is on the outside. No, that won't do, only a true Whovian would know what that means." She thought a minute. "It is blue and white and sort of looks like a British telephone booth but not red. It is a police call box. Mine is about the size of a nine-volt battery."

William scratched his head and looked even more confused. Cara sighed. "It's a flash drive with all my artwork on it." Cara said sarcastically.

"Looks like a phone booth?" William asked. Cara nodded and held up a hand separating her finger and thumb, "About this big."

"Oh is it this thing? I didn't know what this thing was." William went to the kitchen and picked up what looked like a miniature police call box off the counter tossing it to Cara.

"Yes, that's it, my Tardis." Cara said. "I would die if I lost this. I will show you what the real Tardis is, well real in that it is on a television show from England called Doctor Who. We can watch it online."

William shook his head still confused. Girls and women would always be a mystery to him but especially teenage girls. They are the most amazing and perplexing creatures on the planet. They say one thing and mean something completely different. All the while they expect people to know what they are saying and read their minds in between attacks of hysteria, crying, laughing and speaking these foreign words. This one, Cara, was the most confounding one he had met thus far.

Cara tossed the small Tardis in to her purse. William noticed the bag had a photo printed on it of a rather nerdy looking man wearing a red bow tie and holding a silver stick in his hand. No flowers and unicorns for this girl, he thought, but at least she wasn't wearing blue. Cara dressed in cut off denim shorts and a beige tank top slipped black flip flops on to her feet.

They went to the lobby and walked out to the curb where a yellow convertible was waiting with the top down. William opened the passenger's side door and got in.

"What are you waiting for?" he said over his shoulder to Cara.

"Are you serious?" she asked.

"You have your license, right?" he asked knowing she did, "and you can drive a standard?"

"Yes!" she said excitedly.

"Then let's go" he said.

Cara jumped in the sports car and started the engine. She beamed over at William who nodded. She put the car in gear and put her foot down on the accelerator. They drove down the beach road that paralleled the shore. Cara watched as the condos flew past. She was careful not to speed in the car that was more than capable of zooming reckless people to their demise.

"Pull into that store." William said. Cara steered into the almost full parking lot of a store that had a sign that read, The Curiosity Shop out front. It must be a good store. The parking lot was full of cars with tags from all over the country, Cara thought. "Interesting" Cara said as she turned off the motor.

She walked in and said it again. The store was a combination souvenir shop, hardware store and grocery store. There was the typical tourist objects and apparel, including the My friends went to Perdido Key and all I got was this shirt section. In addition, there were key chains, shot glasses and other mementos with seashells and flamingos on them. The other side of the shop was groceries like milk, bread, eggs and other essentials. There were two aisles of hardware. Hammers, duct tape, nails and other hardware paraphernalia lined the wall.

Just when Cara thought the place couldn't get any more curious she saw the prolific wine section. Fine wines from all over the world were represented. There were Bardolino from the Veneto Region of Italy, Cabernet Sauvignon, Pinot Noir, Merlot and others from France. There was a wide selection of American wines. Also, there was an entire section of local wineries. Cara was truly impressed. She picked up a bottle of a local white wine and a bottle of her mother's favorite Apothic Red.

"Here" she said to William "These will do."

"What do you know about wine?" he asked, "You are sixteen years old."

"My grandfather was an amateur connoisseur of wine. He made sure I knew what was good and what goes with what food." she shrugged.

Cara chose a keychain with a dangle shaped like a palm tree hanging from it and a beach towel with a seaside sunset scene. She placed them and the wine on the counter.

"May I see your identification please?" asked an elderly man with happy eyes.

"Oh, she is with me." William said.

"Hi Mr. Porter." The man exclaimed.

"Mr. Trimble, how have you been?" William said firmly shaking the man's hand.

"Great. As you can see business is steady here on the Key." The store owner said.

"This is my friend Cara. I brought her and her mother to have a few days in paradise." William said.

"Well I hope you enjoy your stay miss. Come back to see me when it isn't so busy." Mr. Trimble said motioning to the long line of customers that was forming behind William and Cara. "Sure, we will." William said as he and Cara left the store.

Cara got back into the driver's seat and continued down the beach road. William told her to turn at the next left onto River Rd. She did and slowed down. The road curved to the right. William pointed to a red clay road that went in between trees. "Turn in there and stop."

He said. Cara did as William instructed and stopped, turning off the motor.

"What are we doing here?" she asked.

"Listen I am going to show you something that you can tell your mom about later. I need you to promise me that no matter what happens you will have an open mind. Accept it as is. Do not try to analyze it or figure it out just receive what you see as truth. Do you think you can do that?"

"I will try William, but you are being very strange," she said. "You aren't taking me to some crazy backwoods snake handling church, are you?"

"Lord no" he said smiling. "Actually, the complete opposite. Let's go."

William clutched Cara by the hand and lead her down the dirt road a bit and then he turned off on to a dim path in to the trees. He was careful to push branches away from her so that her bare legs do not get scratched up. Cara started to wonder what exactly was this crazy man up too. She was hoping for some sort of touristy vacation day playing mini golf, swimming or even a day at an aquarium. She wasn't really dressed for a day of hiking. If you could call what they were doing walking through the brush of woods as hiking.

Just when Cara was about to say she had had enough the path opened to a clearing of plush grass in a shade of jade that Cara had never seen in real life before. Around the glade were tall trees. The shrubs and trees made a semicircle around where they are standing. Then Cara saw them, the markings in the bark. They were old but still distinct. The shapes were abstract and deliberate, not something at just appeared in nature. Cara walked over to the closest tree and traced the symbols with her finger. To her surprise the grooves were warm to her touch. She started to take a step into the circle. William abruptly grabbed her arm and stopped her from taking another step.

"Wait." He said a little more sternly than he intended to. "No, don't step on the mound." He points at the ground that was a slightly raised mound from the circle cut out of trees and sloped towards a small pond.

"What kind of trees are these?" Cara asked.

"Cedar and they are old trees." William said. "The marks were left by the original inhabitants of this island. They were native Americans called the Penzacolians. The Timucua, the Apalachee, the Calusa, and many tribes whose names are not as widely known like the Penzacolains, all followed very explicit burial practices. Many people were interned in burial mounds and temple mounds. The marks on the trees were meant to guide the spirits of the warriors to the afterlife."

"So, this is your idea of a fun day in a resort town, visiting an old grave yard." Cara asked William.

"It's much more than that. Come with me. Follow in my steps ok?" William gripped her hand again as he carefully guided her around the edge of the tree line over to a pond. Then through the trees to another open area with a larger pond and a similar circle of trees. The small lake had a pier that jetted out across the water.

"This might have been the site where the royal family is buried. The markings are different on some trees and the lake is bigger." William explained. "This way." He walked out on to the boarded walkway over the lake. Cara followed him. The boards creaked under their feet. At the end, they stood peering out over the water. The water was softly moving lapping gently glistening in the sunlight. William backed up as Cara took off her sandals and sat down on the boards and put her feet down into the water. "It is really pretty here." She said.

A hummingbird darted around Cara's head in a flurry of wings. The little bird hovered right in front of Cara's face compelling her to lift her hand, palm up. The bird settled on the offered perch and looked curiously at Cara. Cara held her breath afraid that the slightest movement would scare the little feathered creature away. The bird pecked at her palm and then disappeared.

"Did you see that?" Cara turned and asked William who was nowhere to be seen. Cara shrugged thinking he must be wandering around some place and she turned to face the lake again. The colors of the trees and flowers around the lake reflected vibrant rainbows across the surface of the water. Cara was simply enjoying the peace that she felt sitting swishing her feet in the cool water.

Suddenly the air felt like it was being pulled from her. The birds stopped tweeting and bugs stopped chirping. The silence surrounded her like a thick fog but the day was clear. A scent of vanilla filled her as she struggled to breath in the thin air. Slowly the water began to swirl small at first in a counter clockwise whirlpool liquid cyclone that grew larger. Cara was on her feet looking down into the center of the spiraling water. Something was beginning to emerge from the vortex. Slowly a woman appeared from out of the spinning water and was floating in the air. She was dressed in a flowing robe of white. Her raven black hair was whipping around her face so Cara could not see her at first. Cara thought she should be terrified but the sense of peace she had looking at the water before the woman appeared continued. The peace held her and like being wrapped in the arms of a parent she felt oddly safe.

    The woman lifted her hands palms up and a bundle began to form in them. It was a baby swaddled in a pink blanket. The woman looked down at the child her face still shielded. A pair of big unattached gnarly looking monster hands appeared from nowhere and snatched the child from the woman. The woman screamed. The sound was screeching and sorrowful. Her hair lifted and left her face. Cara got a good look at the woman's face as she let out a scream of her own. The woman's face was the same as Alison's. Cara was instantly terrified and she turned to run slamming right in to William.

"Whoa there. I've got you" he said.
"Is she gone?" Cara said hiding her face in to his chest.

"Who Cara? We are the only people out here." William said as Cara slowly lifted her face and looked over her shoulder at the lake. The lake was still. The woman was gone.

"You left me." Cara said tears streaming down her face.

"What are you talking about? I have been standing right here watching you." William looked at her confused. "Let's go." Cara pleaded.

Once they returned to the car, William drove away and spoke calmly to Cara. "What happened? What did you see?" Cara told him about the woman. She began to tremble as she described the woman's face. Cara struggled to find the words to explain what transpired or why it happened. All she knew was it did happen. William listened intently and waited for Cara to finish before he spoke.

"I told you there is magic here. I think it was a sign, maybe even a warning." William said.

"A sign? From who? God? Satan?" Cara exclaimed. "And how does a rational Christian man like you believe in such hocus-pocus witchy stuff?"

"It is spirituality, Cara not a religious thing at all. God is infinite. He can use whatever spiritual avenues he wants to get to us." William answered. Cara shook her head.

"I don't know what the hell it was or why it happened. All I know is that it did. I saw it myself."

"I know what you saw was real I experienced it myself. This place is magic Cara. That is why I wanted to bring you and your mother here. This island can heal even the most broken relationship. Just open your heart to it." William said. "At first I thought it was not true. Then I realized I was wrong and it is from God."

They drove in silence. They went back into the condo to find Alison and Faith sitting in the living room surrounded by shopping bags chatting and laughing. Cara half smiled and walked right past them straight to her room.

"How was your day?" William asked the retail scavengers.

"It was amazing. Thank you so much William. I have no idea how I will ever repay you." Alison said. "How was your day? What did you two get into?"

"Don't change the subject. You will never repay me. I will not allow it." William said. "Cara and I went exploring and she met a native. I will let her tell you about it later."

"Speaking of meeting natives" Faith interjected picking up the white bag with the blue ribbon swinging it on one finger. "We met one who knows you and very well she said."

"Ah, you met Krystal." William said.

"Um hum" said Faith.

"She was lovely and invited all of us to her house for dinner tomorrow. She insisted on calling you and that it would be fine with you. I agreed we would go. Should I have waited to speak with you or say no?" Alison's phrases fell out of her in a rush.

"No, it's fine." William said. "She and her husband have a wonderful house on the shore. You will love it."

"Husband you say" Alison looks over at Faith with raised eyebrows.

"Whatever. Is she your ex or not?" Faith asked William.

"Not, not really. I had a thing for her but she was and is completely in love with her husband." William defended.

"So, she was a married woman you had a crush on?" Faith pushed.

"No, they weren't married when she and I met. Look it is a long story and I will fill you two in but not right now." William said and walked out of the room.

"Wow I hit a nerve." Faith said.

"Shut up will you." Alison said and they both burst into laughter.

Chapter Twenty Two

Alison and William had spent the next day on the beach. The waves were beautiful and the temperature was perfect. Alison let the salt water caress her skin as she slowly submerged herself into the water. It was surprisingly warm. She liked how the waves rocked her body back and forth soothingly her nerves. After the swim, they had a picnic lunch of sandwiches from a local deli. William had not been too talkative. Alison was worried that Faith had really offended him by questioning him about his friendship with Krystal.

"I am sorry for Faith last night. She sometimes does not know when to stop talking." Alison said over lunch.

"It's ok. She is just looking out for you." William said. "Like I said. I did have a thing for Krystal, but she was not the woman God had for me. Krystal belongs to her husband and has since she was twelve years old."

"Wow that is amazing. Not many people have a life long relationship or love like that." Alison said.

"Well they had problems too. It isn't my story to tell." William said.

"I thought she was very nice." Alison said. "but she didn't seem like your type."

William laughed. "How could you possibly know what my type is?"

"I don't I guess. She seemed uptight." Alison said.

"Oh, in the store? Yes, she can be. More OCD than uptight. She will be more relaxed tonight. When you see them, Krystal and her husband together you will understand why she and I would never have worked out." William clarified. "If you want to make an instant friend, wear something ocean blue."

"I can do that." Alison smiled. "Let's go for another swim." She stood up, grasped his hand and pulled him to his feet. They splashed each other like children as they bounced up and down with the waves. Alison timed a perfect splash right in William's face as a wave crashed in to them. Seeking revenge, he seized her by the waist, picked her up and tossed her in to the water where she sunk like a rock. William gripped her again and yanked her up above the water. She popped up laughing and sputtering water. He pulled her on to his knee and they clung to each other. He wiped her wet hair off her face. She smiled and licked the salt water off her lips. God I want to kiss her, He thought, no I need to kiss her. It was taking all he had not to devour her. She sensed his need and enfolded her arms around his neck snaking her fingers in his hair. She pulled his face to hers. Slowly she kissed him. Her lips velvety smooth on his. He pulled her body into his. The flimsy fabric of her bikini against his bare chest made it possible for him to feel the points of her nipples. The sensation caused his male anatomy to strongly respond.

"Oh Alison, if I could I would take you to that beach and make love to you right here in the sand." William said as she pulled her mouth from his.

"Why don't you?" She said reaching down inside his swim trunks and encircling his member with her hand.

"I can't break my oath to God, Alison. You are beautiful and sexy. I want you more than I can put in to words." He confessed.

"I can tell." She said with a wicked grin as she squeezed him then let go removing her hand. "I don't want God to strike me with lightning or something equally horrible for making you break your promise." He laughed and hugged her.

"Let's go."

"Come on in." Krystal Sabine said as she opened the door to Alison, Cara and William later that evening.

"Your home is beautiful." said Cara.

Krystal smiled as she led them in to a huge room that was a kitchen on one end with a wall of glass doors on the other side with a living room and dining room area in between. Cara and Alison were immediately drawn to the glass doors that were opened to the shore.

"Oh, my goodness. I would love to live here." Cara gasped.

"Me too" agreed Alison. "This place is incredible."

"Magical." Cara said as she and Alison walked through the open door to the deck.

"Yes indeed," said a man standing on the deck. "Hi, I'm Brendan."

"Hi" said both ladies in unison.

He reached out for Alison grasping her small hand in his. "Oh no, we are huggers here."

Brendan pulled her to him and hugged her tight and released her.

"Here." Alison handed him the bottle of red wine. "I'm William's friend, Alison Lawson and this is my daughter Cara."

"Thank you and yes Cara it is magical here." Brendan smiled.

"Oh, I know. I saw it for myself." Cara said and turned to the water. "You are so lucky to live here."

"We are lucky. William saved our house. If it wasn't for him we would be someplace else." He said.

Alison looked in to the kitchen area where Krystal and William were smiling and talking. She saw that there was something between the two and what she saw she did not like.

"How long have you known William?" Brendan asked causing Alison to spin around.

"Not long" she said. "A few weeks."

"I see." He said. "He must like you a lot to bring you to Florida."

"We like him too." Alison said.

"Yea he is going to save my grandma's house too. I love staying at my grandma's house" Cara said sounding every bit a child.

Brendan and Cara turned to look at the waves crashing just a few feet past the deck lapping on the sugar white sand. Alison took a step closer too but kept a sideways glance into the kitchen where Krystal was opening and closing drawers, cabinets and cupboards in the kitchen. She was obsessively looking for something. Brendan said quietly to himself just barley loud enough where Cara and Alison could hear him. "Third drawer on the left." Alison still looking in to the kitchen sees Krystal stop, stand still for a second then reach for the third drawer on the left of the stove pulling out the corkscrew wine opener. Krystal said something to William, then she walked out to the deck, kissed Brendan lightly on the lips and took the bottle of wine from his hand. She turned and walked back into the house without a word.

Cara and Alison looked at Brendan then at Krystal and back to Brendan. "What the hell?" Alison said shocked.

Brendan chuckled softly, "It's what we do. Cara do you want a soda or wine?

"Soda please." Cara said. "I'm only sixteen."

"Good. I will take a Jack and Coke." Brendan said and pointed in to the kitchen. Alison looked in and saw Krystal carrying a glass of wine and a glass of soda.

"Here you go Alison." Krystal said walking out onto the deck handing the wine to Alison and the glass of soda to Cara. "I will be back with your jack and Coke, love. Didn't want to spill it trying to carry three drinks." Again, she kissed him lightly and walked back into the house.

"Holy shit." Cara said.

"Holy shit is right" Alison said blushing "Sorry, but this place is magic."

Brendan laughed a deep belly laugh. "It is magic here, however, what Krys and I have is a deep long standing connection. Not magic at all. We have been that was since we were kids. That is how it is when God chooses your mate. When you accept it and when you are with the one you are meant to share this life with there is no greater peace."

"Did she hear you?' Cara asked intrigued

"Sort of. It is like we live in each other's heads."

Brendan turned looked in the house. "Like now, I have an ache in the back of my head." He said rubbing his skull. "She is getting a headache because she hasn't drunk enough water today." Krystal was in the kitchen chatting with William. She opened a cabinet, pulled out a bottle of aspirin, filled a tall glass with water and popped two pills in her mouth. She then reached up and rubbed the back of her skull in the same place that Brendan had just rubbed on his.

"Amazing." Alison said mesmerized.

"I want a love like that," Cara said

"Me too" Alison said. She realized that there was no chance that William and Krystal had anything serious between them. The woman in the kitchen belonged to the man looking in the window with Alison. Brendan watched Krystal with pure devotion on his face. He looked at her as if she were a goddess.

William and Krystal came out to the deck each with plates and food stuff in their hands. There was a table and chairs that Krystal suggested they sit around, as she placed plates of salad on the table. They all sat and Brendan nodded at William.

"Shall I say grace?" William said. Everyone bowed their heads and held hands. Cara was between Krystal and Brendan. His hand is super-hot, Cara thought and her hand is ice cold. Cara thought that was one more thing that made those two perfect for each other.

William said a quick prayer and they all began to eat. Cara watched Krystal and Brendan pour salad dressing on their salads in unison. Then they picked up salt and pepper shakers one each. Shook out the contents on their respected plates and handed the shakers to each other repeated the motion. They picked up their forks, hers in her right hand his in his left and the took synchronized bites of salad. Cara looked over at Alison. Alison shook her head.

"I think we freaked out our guests." Brendan said. William laughed.

"It is a bit unnerving being with you two. Alison, this is easier here than going out to dinner with them, I can promise you that." William said.

"Why is that?' Alison asks.

"We order the same things." Brendan said.

"Without looking at the menu" Krystal said.

"They do it without talking to each other." William said. "Watch this." William reached in his shirt pocket and pulled out a pen. He handed it to Krystal. "Write a number, any number. Make it difficult, say a multi digit." She smiled and wrote a number down on a napkin carefully hiding it with her hand. William handed the pen to Brendan. He wrote a number. Krystal handed the napkin to Cara and Brendan handed his to Alison.

"Ok, you two say the number at the same time. Alison and Cara both said, "1968"

"See?" William said. "It's insane."

Everyone laughed.

"Its magic. Like the woman in the lake." Cara said. "I thought I imagined it but no, I really saw her." The adults around the table silently stared at Cara. "What? I saw her. I did."

Krystal patted the girl's hand. "Yes, you did. It is good luck to have seen her."

Cara looked over at Alison, "See, I am not crazy?" Cara had spent the better part of the afternoon explaining to her mother what she had seen at the lake. Alison thought it had to be a stress induced episode.

After dinner William suggested that he and Alison go for a walk on the beach.

"I want to go too." Cara asked.

"Hey, how about you let William and your mom go this time." Krystal said.

"Yeah, you can play a card game with us." Brendan suggested.

William looked over at Krystal and mouthed his thanks. Krystal smiled and nodded.

William and Alison walked out to the shore. She instantly kicked off her shoes and left them on the last step of the deck. William grabbed her hand and pulled her so her feet were on the edge of the crashing waves. She laughed and kicked water at him. He splashed her back. They laughed and continued to walk.

"So, Cara thinks she saw some mysterious ghost?" Alison said.

"She did see her. I was with Cara when she saw the woman in the lake." William said solemnly.

"Um hum. I do not believe in all that." Alison said.

"Do you believe in God, Alison?" William asked. Alison answered without thinking. "Yes, just not that he cares about us. I guess you can say I am more of a deist than anything else. I mean come on. Why would a creator that made all this happen" she said making a wide motion towards the rolling waves "why would he care about a lowly person like me? I am sure he has something better to do."

William shook his head, "No you are his most valuable creation. Well you and the rest of the people on the planet. To me you are one of his most treasured." He stopped and clutched her in to his arms. He rubbed her face taking her chin in his hands. Slowly he bent his head and kissed her. Alison melted into his embrace. "We better get back." William said. Alison's face blanched white.

"William, I just thought those exact words. Not funny William." Alison suddenly angry. "I am not going to change my entire belief system just because of the fantasy of this place. It is not real William. You cannot read my thoughts. What the hell?"

"Relax Alison. It was a coincidence. That's all. Let's go." William said.

"Wait, no. I have to ask you." Alison turned to look William straight in the face. "Why exactly did you promise your celibacy to God? No man I know would go without sex very long much less vow to be celibate until marriage."

William took off his hat and ran his hand through his hair. He turned and threw his hands up in the air and began to pace. "I am not ready to have this conversation." He said looking up.

"Sit." He said pointing over to a smooth weathered log that was laying at the base of a large sand dune. Something in his tone made Alison obey without question. She could see his face wrinkled with pent up anger. She was sorry she had pried into his life. It wasn't really any of her business and this man had been so kind to her, Cara and her mother. She really shouldn't have asked him. William looked down at Alison and let out an exasperated growl. He turned on his heel, "Really God?" He shouted. "Ugh!" He stomped back to Alison.

"I'm sorry…It's ok…you really do not have to tell me." Alison stammered.

"Oh, no sweet girl." William said dropping to his knees. "This is between me and God. He wants me to tell you and I am not ready. Truth is I will never be completely ready to tell anyone. I have only confided in one other person, Krystal Sabine."

Alison smiled, "Ok, then don't tell me."

"Shut up." William said. "I will tell you the story."

Chapter Twenty Three

William Porter met Evette in a bar. Not a dump on the corner of any street in any neighborhood, but a local hang out none the less. William was playing pool with a friend and was running the table. He had recently been promoted to lead in the sales department and was celebrating the way men do with booze, pretty women and taking trash talk from his friends. William lined up his next shot. "Six ball left corner pocket." he said as looked down the length of his cue stick. Just as he took the shot, his vision was filled with red silk and skin. He looked up to see a tall blond woman standing slightly leaning on the side of the pool table across from him in a red dress with a slit traveling up one thigh. He blinked twice as if trying to decide if she was a real woman or a hallucination from the drinks he had consumed.

"Oh, I am so sorry I ruined your shot." She purred.

"Ah, it's ok I was finished anyway." William said with a sheepish grin on his face.

The two of them spent the entire evening talking and laughing. William was smitten by Evette's wit and charm. Theirs was a classic whirlwind romance. It only took William a couple of months to buy an engagement ring.

Looking back, he should have seen the warnings. He should have known that she was not all that she appeared to be. He was about to propose to a woman who had an excuse every time he asked about meeting her family. William couldn't wait to introduce her to his mother, in fact he had taken her to his mother's house for dinner week five of their relationship. Not only did he take her to his mother's house for dinner but it was Sunday dinner at that. Then there was the mystery of her closet. She had an entire second closet in her spare guest room of women's business suits. As far as William knew she never had a real job. He asked her about the closet and she blew him off with an, "I may want to work one day" excuse that William thought sounded plausible to him. Besides what he knew about women you could write on a cocktail napkin and still have room for your glass.

    He wasn't sure how Evette would react to a proposal. She never let William stay at her apartment overnight. She claimed that she could not sleep with anyone else in the bed with her. He even offered to sleep down the hall if she would just agree to let him stay the entire night, His plan was to sneak back in to her bed after she had fallen to sleep and in the morning, tell her that she was being silly. He would explain that she had slept with him right there the whole night. Evette never gave him the chance to try this armature psychology on her, but William thought he would be able to work on sleeping in the same bed after she accepted his proposal.

When the big night came William planned the perfect proposal. William took Evette to a theater where an improv group was performing a modernized version of the old fairy tale about the princess and the pea. William contacted the stage manager because Evette had told William that fairy tale was one of her all-time favorites from childhood. He proposed after the cast's curtain call by having the director call Evette to the stage and William proposing right there in front of everyone. He had a special note added into the playbill as a keepsake of the proposal.

He approached Evette standing center stage and got on one knee. She looked shocked and told him to wait. She ran off stage. William could see her on her cell phone but could not hear her conversation He assumed she was calling her mother and father. She looked petrified. Just as William was about to stand up off his one sad knee, tell Evette never mind and withdraw his proposal, she returned all giggling and happy to say yes.

After Evette accepted William's proposal things got even more strange. She seemed uninterested when William tried to discuss wedding plans she avoided the conversation. This evasion went on for months.

William began to suspect she may even be having an affair. Evette would disappear for hours with little or no explanation as to where she had been. Then one day it all became glaringly obvious exactly what Evette Johnson had been up to.

William had been in a huge corporate takeover deal that was set to yield him millions in commission. He had convinced Evette to go with him to New York for a mini vacation. He would spend one day petitioning for this deal and the rest of the time negotiating a wedding date out of the woman he loved. The day before the big meeting he took Evette out to one of the prominent night clubs in the city. She spent most of the night dancing with other men and flirting. William sat at the bar watching. As the night wore on he got crazy drunk and more jealous. Eventually he had enough and picked her up over his shoulder and took her back to their hotel room. He demanded she pick a date and stick to it. He manhandled her and ripped off her clothes. What they did was not love making it was primal sex. He claimed what was his.

As William told this story to Alison, his face fell. She could see the remorse all over him. She reached up and touched his arm. "Oh William." she said.

He shrugged her off. "No, I deserved some of what happened. I was an animal to her. I did not rape her. She wanted it but I hurt her physically Alison." He said.

"The next morning, she was gone and my files for the deal closing were gone too. I didn't put it together about her being a liar and the missing files at first. When I got to the meeting with the executives to handle the merger. She was there already but on the other side of the conference table. She had signed the company with her firm. That had been another lie; I had no idea she even had a job, much less at the competing firm. I also had no idea she was using me to find out the details of the merger for her company. She had played me. Evette was, is a corporate spy. She never loved me." William looked in to Alison's eyes. His were filled with tears that mirrored her own.

"I promised God that if he let me get through the humiliation and keep my job that I wouldn't drink anymore, at least I would never get drunk again. I also promised that I would not sleep with another woman until I was married. I swore I would treat that woman like a princess, no a queen with all the respect I could manage." William took a deep breath.

Alison's head was spinning. She never would have guessed that the William she knew would be capable of being a drunk mad man.

She understood being possessive of those you love and wanting to keep them to yourself. Her situation with Cara was different but she felt every bit insanely selfish of her daughter.

"Do you understand Alison why I can't have you the way you want me to. I have to be sure that when I do have sex again it is with the woman who God has for me to marry." William said.

"Yes, I understand William and I am not the marrying type." Alison said. "It's not me William. I am not the girl God has for you."

Somewhere off in the distance on the wind William heard a small voice. "She is wrong. She is the one." William grabbed Alison in to his arms and kissed her hard. She was stiff at first then complied. Their kiss grew hungry and fervent. "What if you're wrong?" he whispered in to her mouth.

Chapter Twenty Four

The flight home was uneventful and quiet. Cara sat between William and Alison both of whom haven't said more than two words to each other while loading on to the plane. Cara could feel the tension between them so she tried to distract them with small talk. All she managed to get out of them was the occasional yes and uh huh. She was desperate to find out what was going on with them but the miserable look on her mother's face kept her from asking. When they got back to Savannah and got to the tarmac William had a car waiting. He walked with them to the car and opened the door. Alison said thank you and climbed in. Cara shook her head and flung her arms around William's neck.

"Thank you for the amazing vacation" Cara said. "Will we see you at home later?"

"No, your mother wants me to give her some space, so I will go to the hotel and leave for Nashville tomorrow." He said.

Really? What happened between you two?" she asked.
"Nothing I can talk about." He said.

Cara gave him a disbelieving looking. "Sure, I can tell. Nothing happened. That is why you two haven't spoken to each other all day." Cara said. She turned to the car and opened the door. "Get out." She demanded of her mother. "Get out of the car. You are not leaving this man like this. He deserves at least a hug. Mother! Get out of the Car." Cara shouted when Alison turned her head and looked away not moving from where she was seated in the back of the car. Cara stood hands on her hips not moving. She looked over at William who shrugged at her. "Ugh really mother?" Cara said "I am sorry William. I tried."

"It's ok, when she is ready to talk to me she will, it's ok," He said.

Cara climbed in to the car and William watched the car begin to drive away. Abruptly the car stopped, the door flung open and Alison jumped out. She ran full speed to William and hurled herself in to his open arms. "I am not perfect, I am really rather a mess. I'm a lazy housekeeper and I am bad with money. I can cook some things and burn others. I drink too much, sometimes." Pausing to take a breath she looked up at William whose face was plastered with a silly grin. "OK, ok, I drink too much all the time. I won't make a good house wife at all. Not that I am saying I want to be your wife. All I am saying is that if you want to, I am willing to see where this, whatever this is we have is going to go. I might go crazy on you sometimes and I will be demanding of your attention, but if you want to try then let's try to see what happens."

Alison paused to take another breath and before she could let out the next barrage of words William scooped her up on to his arms and kissed her and hugged her in a giant bear hug.

"Let's give it a shot." He said.
She smiled and hugged him back. "I will see you soon. I must go to my office in Nashville. Will you wait for me Alison?" he asked.

"Yes, I will wait, but don't make me wait too long William Porter." Alison said.

"That's more like it!" Cara shouted jumping up and down excitedly.

The next few days creeped by for Alison and Cara as they waited for William to return from Nashville. Life was back to normal. Cara went to school and Alison went to work. William called them every evening and texted Alison several times a day. It did not help them miss each other any less. It made being apart feel worse for both of them.

William was pacing around his office when Mark come in to see him. They hugged and Mark laughed at William.

"What has you all fired up my friend?" He asked William.

"It's that woman, Alison." William confided.

Mark burst into a big belly laugh. "A woman? You don't say?"

"Not funny Mark" William said. "I have done what I said couldn't be done. What I said would never happen has happened. I have fallen head over heels for this girl. I just thought I loved Krystal Sabine, that was puppy love, or straight out lust compared to how I feel for Alison. Mark, I can't stand another night of not having her in my bed and in my life. I need her here every day. I crave her like a fat kid craves cake."

Mark patted his friend on the back. "I am not surprised. What did she say when you told her about your pact with the big guy?"

"That is the thing Mark, I told her the entire story and she didn't run. She was scared. She said she wasn't good enough for me. Can you believe that garbage? That beautiful woman thought she was less than perfect for me when in reality she is more than I could have ever hoped for." William said.

"Boss is she a Christian?" Mark asked. Williams face fell. "No, she said she wasn't. She believes in God. She isn't an atheist, so there is hope."

"It isn't my place sir, but I have to tell you the truth. You know you can count on me to be the one to always tell you like it is, you can't marry her if she isn't a Christian, boss." Mark said solemnly.

William sighed. "We will just have to see what God says about that Mark." William said knowing that his friend was telling him the truth.

"I have news too sir." Mark said and he began to explain his recent trip to Florida with Lauren. He told William that there was something amiss with her family and he was determined to find out what it was so that the woman he loved would commit to him.

"This is where you come in, Sir. I know her sister has a secret. It is one that keeps a cloud of darkness over Lauren. It sent her to a shrink a couple of times a month and it prevents her from settling down with me. She is certain that it will cause me to leave her if I found out."

"Has she said that, Mark?" William asked.

"Not in those words but in others. Will you help me?" Mark pleaded.

"Of course, of course." William said, "It seems we have our work cut out for us with these two woman of ours."

"That we do sir, that we do." Replied Mark. "I am headed back to Florida in the morning. I do not want to be too far from Lauren for too long." William smiled a knowing smile at Mark. Yeah, he has it as bad as I do, William thought.

That night William was laying on his bed and he called Alison. He waited until he knew she would be home and in her pajamas drinking wine. He was hoping she would be in a light mood wanting to talk. She answered the phone on the first ring.

"Hi you." William could hear the smile in her voice when Alison answered the phone.

"Hi yourself. I need to ask you a couple of questions." He said.

"Oh no this sounds serious. Are you having second thoughts about us?" she asked hurriedly.

"Hush, please and let me ask you this. I know you said you aren't a religious girl, but have your feelings or thoughts changed since we got back from Florida?" The brave and strong cowboy timidly asked.

"I don't know William." Alison said. What she didn't tell him was that she had been thinking a lot about God and his role in the lives of people. She thought that surely the magic at the beach had to come from some place. It could just be an anomaly or maybe even a miracle? What unnerved her was that she had thought about talking to William but chickened out when it came to actually phoning him and telling him her thoughts. How did he know that she was thinking these things not a half hour before he called her?

She continued. "I mean I was thinking that the magic was not a complete hoax. I saw it in action when Krystal and Brendan did the crazy mind thing. How is it possible that the things just happened? Then there is Cara who is convinced that she saw the woman of the lake. She even told her friends at school and risked teenage ridicule and rejection about it, so she really believes she saw what she saw. All that got me thinking about God, sure."

"I just want to know where your head is Alison, that's all." William said nervously and Alison could hear the insecurity in his voice.

"Does this change things for you about us William?" She asked.

"To be honest Alison, if we get to the point where we are considering marriage, yes it does change things. Right now, we are just starting out. I say we just let God have his way with us and see where this ends up going ok?" William said.

"Do you think we will get to that point?" she asked in a mirrored reflected timid voice of his.

"Yes, I do. We will get there." William said. "Good night my sweet girl."

They both hung up their phones and simmered in their thoughts of each other. She of him and God. He of her and God. Both contemplating the reality of the situation. Were they a match made in heaven or a fleeting fancy of earth bound mystical happenstance? Only time could answer that for them. Time was the one thing they had plenty of between them. At least that is what they thought.

Chapter Twenty Five

Lauren sat in a chair looking at a tall wall of windows. The office is bright and lined with bookshelves full of books. The rug under her feet was thick and squishy. Lauren slipped her feet out of her sandals and wiggled her toes in the soft yarn of the rug. The door behind her opened and Lauren forced her feet quickly back in to her shoes.

"I am sorry for keeping you waiting." The voice of Corina Santo, Lauren's psychiatrist, flows in to the room. "Let's see, where were we?" Dr. Santo all business flips through the papers in the chart she has in her hands as she sits across from Lauren behind the big wooden desk. "Ah, yes, we were talking about your sister."

Lauren slips her feet back into the rug. Gosh it is soft, she thinks.

"Lauren?"

Lauren looks up and smiles. "I just don't see what my sister has to do with me. I mean, really, what does she have to do with my issues and why I can't set a wedding date?"

"Well Lauren it is my job to figure that out." Doctor Santo said, "so just relax and tell me about Traci."

"My sister has always been a little off. She was the weird kid in the neighborhood. When we went grocery shopping with my mom she had to line up the cans in the cart by category then size. At the checkout she did the same thing on the conveyor. She always had no less than six toothbrushes at any given time and they were everywhere. When she committed her first suicide attempt she was only eleven years old. She had started her period at school and mom had to pick her up. She has soiled her clothes and every one of her friends laughed at her.

Traci went home and got in the shower. She took a long time so mom went to check on her. She had two perfectly equal two inch long cuts on both wrists. She spent several weeks at the hospital. Things were different after that. On the rare occasion that we were allowed to go outside and ride our bikes I had to stay with her. Traci was never left alone. Can you imagine never being alone?" Lauren shivered a bit. "I love, loved my sister, but everyone loved Traci. They should. She is perfect. My mom loved her so much she wanted me to be just like her. Mom still does. I remember the worst suicide attempt when we were in our early twenties. It was awful."

"Mom was pacing the waiting room floor. She was dressed like she had just stepped out of Ladies Home Journal article about working mothers. She was wearing a crisp pressed black skirt, a white buttoned-down shirt and shiny patent leather pumps."

"What's wrong with that?" Doctor Santo asks.

"It was three in the morning. Dad and I were in our pajamas. I even had my fluffy bunny slippers on. My mother would never have been seen in public without her makeup on and be fully dressed. This day I have no idea how she got her makeup on so fast." Lauren pondered.

The memory played in Lauren's head like a movie. She could see her mother, Marion Barton, pacing the floor in the hospital waiting room. Her mirror like shoes clicking on the tile floor. Lauren's father, Fred Barton pouring himself a cup of strong hours old coffee and running his hand through is sparse hair making it stand on end.

"What is taking so damn long?" Marion complains "I have so much to do today to get ready for my dinner party tomorrow. They just need to decide if we are taking her home or if they are admitting her. Fred, did you remember to call the caterers? Are they going to have the fresh fish I want?"

Fred takes a long slow sip of the coffee. "Yes dear I called them. I asked about fish. They said they have grouper."

"No, Fred I want flounder or salmon. I think maybe shrimp as well. What do you think Lauren?" Marion asked.

Lauren yawned and stretched in the chair. "Mother I don't care what kind of fish you have at your precious party. I think it is sad that you are talking about fish when my sister is in the emergency room." Lauren stood and walked over to the coffee pot. "We can't have a party now mother. Sissy will be down for a few days after this if they even let her come home."

Marion strides to stand next to Lauren. "I am not canceling the party." She hisses. "Sister in the hospital or not. It is tradition. Our friends expect it before we go to the lake house. It is the official summer kickoff party. Your sister is fine. All she needs is a little rest. She is just stressed out about summer classes. She would be sad if we did not have the party. What is wrong with you Lauren?"

"Nothing is wrong with me mother," Lauren snarls back at her mother. "I am thinking about what might be best for my sister. Someone should think of what is best for her. Where is the doctor? I will find out what is going on. Come with me dad?"
Fred stands to join his youngest daughter.

"For Christ's sake, sit down the both of you. I will go find the doctor. She is my daughter." Marion turns on her heel and stomps her shoes down the hallway. Less than five minutes later she was back with a self-satisfied smirk on her face.

"Did you find the doctor?" Fred asked looking up from his second cup of coffee.

"Of course, the doctors said we can take her home. I will go help Traci get dressed." Marion continued.

"I will come with you mom," Lauren said.

"Absolutely not. I will help my daughter myself." Marion strode out of the room before Lauren or Fred could protest.

The doctor entered the waiting room a few minutes later. He shook Fred's hand. "So tell us the truth doctor. It's bad this time right?" Fred asked.

"Yes, it is. Your daughter needs help. I can't get through to your wife. She chooses to see it as a temporary illness. If Traci does not get the help she needs she will continue to get worse. She needs an inpatient facility to give her the care she needs to improve. Here" he said and hands Fred his card. "If you can make any headway with your wife, here is my card, call me. Though Traci is technically an adult she will not make this decision on her own. We can guide her, but without her mother's approval it will be difficult."

"Thank you, doctor," Fred answers.

"That is enough for today Lauren." Doctor Santos breaks the spell. "We will pick up here next time." Lauren shakes her head of the fog of the scene that was playing out in her memory as she conveyed the incident to her shrink.

Lauren leaves the office and heads straight to her favorite bar. She calls Mark and tells him she will be late. He asked her how the visit with the doctor went. She simply says ok and tells him she will pick him up at the airport. Then she ends the call.

What she wants is to escape the memories that will not stop now that they are free in her brain. She still has no clue how this will help her. She loves Mark and she will marry him, when she is ready and not a moment before, shrink or no shrink.

Chapter Twenty Six

Mark flew back to Florida. In the car from the airport Lauren and Mark had a heated discussion about where they would stay. After some convincing Lauren won Mark over. They would stay in Lauren's apartment. Mark had wanted to stay at the resort at Lost Key however Lauren insisted that they stay at her place. She thought it was a waste of money to stay in the resort when she had a perfectly cozy apartment in the city. True, it was not someplace grand. Lauren's decorating style was more bohemian than elegant. She laughed when she saw the look on Mark's face when he walked in and looked around her living room. Her main room was full of bright colored fabric covered furniture from every decade. Nothing matched and nothing was new. She furnished her home with flea market finds and hand me down items.

"This is nice." Mark finally said.

"Not what you are used too," Lauren giggled.

"It has a kitchen, bathroom and a bed I assume?" Mark asked.

"Of course," she answered.

"Then it has all we need. When do we see your family." He asked as he watched Lauren's color drain from her face.

"I will see them tomorrow. I am not ready for you to meet them." She said.

"Negative." Mark replies. "You will not go alone. I do not want you out of my sight." Lauren sighed. "We'll see."

That had been a week ago and Mark still had not met Lauren's family. She did take Mark to her therapy appointment just to find out he had already called her doctor. For all she knew Mark has already found out about her family.

As they walked out of the doctor's office Lauren suggested that they go for a ride to the beach. She wanted to sit by the shore and enjoy the sun. Mark thought it was a good idea.

Within an hour they were sitting on the deck of the Reef. They looked through the menu and Mark told Lauren to order for them both so he could go make a phone call. Mark stepped out to the shore and dialed William's number. He answered on the first ring. "Hello my friend, what's going on?" William said.

"I know there is some secret she is hiding." Mark answered.

"She is a woman Mark. They all have secrets. The question is this, are you the one she wants to trust with her secrets." William said. "Where are you at now by the way?"

"Your favorite place, The Reef." Mark said.

"Then why are you on the phone with me? Go, woo that librarian. I will see what I can find out about her sister. Text me all the info you can about her family later, for now what is her sister's name?" William said.

"As you wish, sir. Traci Barton, she is 4 years older than Lauren." Marks said adding his goodbye to William and disconnected the call in the middle of William's waves of laughter.

Mark returned to the table to see a tall glass with a fruity red cocktail in it complete with a miniature umbrella. "What is that?" he asks Lauren.

She smiles, "It is a Perdido Punch. It has tequila, Triple Sec, Rum, Vodka, Gin, Cranberry Juice and a Splash of Sour Mix. Taste it, it's yummy."

Mark takes a small sip. Fruity drinks are not his usual choice. He is more a whisky man, however when your girl orders you a fruity drink you drink the thing. Mark was relieved to see a waitress place a plate full of fried calamari on the table between them. He was afraid his girl had ordered him a salad.

After a few minutes Mark braved asking Lauren about her family again. This time his approach was softer. "So, Lauren, tell me more about your family, what did your father do?" he asked.

"He was an accountant." Lauren said with no elaboration.

"I see." Mark said.

"Look I know you want to know more. I am not ready to tell you more." Lauren said. "I will but not yet." They finished their dinner in silence and there was no more talk about family that night.

A few days later Lauren walked out of Dr. Santo's office with a frown on her face. Lauren's heels clicked down the sidewalk as she made her way down the street. She was not happy with the instructions she had been given.

"He deserves your honesty" Doctor Santo had said about Mark. "If you are going to marry him, be honest, Lauren." She wanted very much to not tell Mark any of her family history, but she knew that was impossible. Doctor Santos insisted she tell him all of it. Lauren wanted to only tell him enough so that he would accept her.

Lauren finally made her way to the apartment where Mark was sitting at the table flipping through some folders and reading documents. Lauren walked up to him and he laid his head on her chest. She ran her fingers through his thick hair. He moaned and relaxed further against her wrapping his arms around her and stroking her back. "Hi" he said into her.

"Hi" she answered. "Ok I will tell you about my family."

"ok, not here." Mark said as he discreetly pushed the papers in to the folder. "Living room, go."

The couple settled on to the sofa. Mark had poured them each a glass of red wine. Lauren took a deep breath and closed her eyes. The memories flooded her conciseness like a tidal wave. She could see the recollections dance in front of her like flickers from the television as when you skim through the channels quickly in the dark of night. She decided it was best to just start talking and not stop until her story was finished, so she began.

The morning after the Barton family had taken Traci to the emergency room, Lauren and her father were sitting at the breakfast table. Lauren looked over her bowl of cereal at the newspaper her father held in front of his face. An occasional grunt came from behind the paper as Fred Barton read the day's news. Lauren wanted to talk to her father but found herself immersed in an advertisement for silver polish. She wondered if it indeed made silver mirror bright.

Shaking her head, she asked her dad, "Is mom still planning on the party tonight?"

"Hum?" said her father with a flick of the paper as he turned the page and continued to read. "Yes honey. She left about an hour ago to speak to the chef."

Lauren reached over and pushed the newspaper out of the way. She looked her father straight in the eyes, "Are you serious? She can't. Traci isn't up to it. She will embarrass mom. She is in no condition to attend a party and you know mom will expect her to be there anyway." Lauren blinks back tears. Fred sighs.

"I know sweetie. I will see what I can do. It is her annual bash. She will not cancel it. Maybe I can convince her that you two girls can skip it." Fred shakes his head at the thought. "She won't like it. No, she won't like it one bit."

"I can get us all packed for the lake house and Sissy can rest." Lauren suggested. "It's all your and mom's stuffy friends anyway."

"You mom's friends mostly" Fred agrees. He looks out the kitchen window framed in yellow and white gingham checked curtains. A silver sports car pulls up the driveway. "There is your mother. Let me get this kitchen cleaned before she orders me to do it. Go check on your sister."

Laurens ran upstairs leaned on the doorframe and looked in on her snoring sister. That sedative must have been a doozy, Lauren thought. "Sissy" Lauren said to her sister in a voice just barely over a whisper. Traci stirred but did not wake up. "Sissy, wake up please." The girl shaped mound of quilts moaned and moved. "Sissy I need to talk to you." Lauren said louder.

"Go away." The bed said. Lauren walked over and sat on the edge of the bed and patted what she thought to be her sister's back.

"Traci, what is it this time?" Lauren asked.

"Lu Lu, go away. I am not talking to you about it and I am not getting up." Traci said and yanked the covers up over her head tighter. Her sister's use of her childhood nickname made Lauren smile and filled her with sadness at the same time.

Just then their mother walks in to the room picking up clothing that is scattered across the floor. "Leave your sister alone Lauren. She needs her rest. I want everyone well rested and smiling for the party." Marion said.

Lauren opens her mouth to protest once more that going to a party is the last thing her sister needs to do. Something in the way Marion looks at Lauren makes her close her mouth. Instead of saying anything, Lauren stands up, rolls her eyes at her mother and backs out of the room.

Marion takes the spot on the bed that Lauren left and pulls the covers down revealing Traci's pale face and red rimmed eyes. The mother pushes a strand of hair from her daughter's face just like she did when she was a little girl. "It is all going to be alright my dear. Everything is fine. You are fine and the party will be amazing. Everything is fine." Marion said trying to convince herself as much as Traci.

The memory was so intense that Lauren had to force it out of her skull. Lauren shook her head as if to shake off the memory. She looked over at Mark. "My mother was, is a controlling person. She is the main reason for mine and my sister's problems."

"I can see that." Mark said softly. "So, did your mother still have a party?"

"oh yes." Lauren said. She took another long drink of her wine and after a deep breath to steady her nerves she continued telling her story to Mark.

The night of the party was clear and perfect as the Barton girls pull up in front of the banquet hall in a rented car. Their mother insisted that they arrive in style and on time, so she arranged a limo to pick them up. The valet, a tall thin boy, opens the door of the car and out of the back seat stands Traci dressed in a velvet gown in a deep shade of green with thin rows of rhinestones strapped across her shoulders. Lauren follows with a rich blue gown of flowing chiffon that touches the top of her feet. Both girls had their hair done in identical French twists knotted up on the back of their heads. On the drive to the party, Lauren had taken all one hundred and forty-two bobby pins out of her hair, brushing the dark waves to lay down her back.

The sisters walk hand in hand in to the large party room full of tables of smiling people most of which are their parents ages and older. The tables are clothed in white with large blue and green centerpieces of flowers in the middle. Lauren is disgusted when she realizes her mother planned their outfits to match the table decor.

Marion spots her girls the instant they enter the room. She glides over to them with a plastic smile on her face. She takes Traci in her arms and hugs her gently giving her non-contact kiss on each cheek. "I thought I told you to get your hair done just like your sister?" Marion said as she let go of Traci and gave Lauren a slight hug.

"You look lovely too, Mother." Lauren said through a clenched smile.

"Come this way girls. I will show you to your table." Marion said spinning on her heels floating across the room. The two sisters followed their mother as she was stopped by guests as they made their way through the party.

Marion was on her stage and was performing like a renowned actress. Even the simplest small talk kept party goers enthralled as she spoke. Eventually the women made it to the destined table. Lauren and Traci sat down facing the band that was playing a popular light jazz song.

With two champagne flutes filled to the brim, one in each hand, a sleek sexy man makes his way over and stops in front of their table. "Hello ladies. Wow, I am sitting at the table with the best view. You two look amazing." He said as he handed a glass first to Traci and then to Lauren. Charles Sebastian grinning leaned over and kissed Traci on the cheek. Lauren looked away.

"Oh my God, should you drink that Traci?" Lauren asked as her sister tipped up the champagne draining the glass.

"Shut up, Lu Lu. I am fine." She said as she set the glass down on the table.

"Let's dance darling." Charles said taking Traci's hand. Lauren's head snapped around as she stared at Traci.

"Traci, you shouldn't. Please don't." Lauren said giving her sister a warning with her eyes.

"I am fine. I love dancing." Traci stands and wraps her arm around her boyfriend's neck. "I love dancing with you the most." She looked back at Lauren, glaring at her.

The night wears on and Lauren sits through most of it alone at the table while Traci and Charles dance only stopping occasionally for a drink. Traci is getting more intoxicated as the hours pass. About four drinks in Traci stands at the front of the room close to the band and sings. Her words are slurred and she stumbles around the room. She snatches a microphone from a shocked band member. Her voice is no clearer with the amplification and Traci doesn't seem to notice. She winks at Charles who laughs nervously. He approaches Traci and tried to get her to hand him the microphone.

"I wanna be loved. Wait, wait that's not how the song goes." Traci mumbles something incoherent then begins to sing louder. She dances over to Charles and begins to do an erotic strip tease dance awkwardly in front of him. Lauren is by her side in a matter of seconds.

"Come on sissy. Let's go home." Lauren pleads with her sister.

"No. I wanna dance for Charles." Traci whines and lifts the hem of her skirt almost waist high.

Marion stomps over to her daughter and whispers harshly. "Stop it. Stop it this instant. What are you doing?"

The music stops. Marion's face is hot with anger and embarrassment. Fred motions for a waiter and tells him to get the car pulled up to the door. Fred sees that his wife is about to explode and it will not be pretty. Lauren and Charles help Traci stay on her feet. Lauren pulls her sister's dress down and the begin to move her toward the door.

Marion addresses the room, "Please eat, dance." She motions to the band. "Play. It is ok. My daughter has had just a little too much to drink. She will be fine. We are sending her home to rest." The band begins to play again.

Lauren pulls her sister towards the door. "This way Sissy. We are going home." Traci pulls away from Lauren.

"No, I wanna sing and dance too. I don't wanna go home."

Charles steps in to help by wrapping Traci in his arms. "It's ok love. We can dance at home."

The room goes silent.

Marion goes to the platform where the band is sitting and grabs a microphone. She clears her throat and before she can say anything there came a shout from Traci.

"Stop it I want to dance, damn it." Charles and Lauren let go of Traci as she yanked away from them. Traci grabs a second microphone and beings to sing. "I wanna be fucked by you, by nobody else but you."

Charles is at her side in an instant. "Honey, that is not how that song goes. You can sing it to me in the car. We want to be alone right?"

Traci smiles and falls in to Charles's awaiting arms. "But I have to tell you something." Traci said in a loud attempt to whisper.

"Ok, love you can tell me in the car." Charles said and pulls her towards the door. Traci puts the microphone to her mouth. "Charles, I'm pregnant."

The color drained from Charles's face and looked at Traci blankly. After a few seconds, he snatched the microphone from her hand and pushed her to the door. Lauren was two steps behind them. Marion clears her throat again nervously. "Please everyone, dance eat. She is fine. Lauren and Charles will take her home." To the band Marion flaps her arms wildly, "Play, play. Now."

The band begins to play an upbeat song as Marion darts around the room encouraging the shocked guests to dance and continue with the party. Charles, Traci and Lauren climb in to the back seat of the awaiting car.

Back on the sofa in Lauren's apartment in Florida, "Wow" Mark says to Lauren and she stops talking to catch her breathe. She nods.

"Yeah, but there is more, Mark much more." She said as dread filled her. She did not want to continue, but she knew if she did not keep going she would not be able to start again.

Lauren's mouth froze. She could not say the words. Despite the banging in her chest that urged her to continue, she did not speak. She did not have the strength in her to tell Mark the story about her sister's baby. She couldn't tell him about the day her sister attempted to commit suicide again; however, that time she was successful.

Chapter Twenty Seven

Cara did not know what to do to help her mother. She knew her mom was unhappy during the weeks since William left. She could not understand why the adults made things so difficult. It was obvious to everyone that they loved each other and were miserable apart. They should just stop being ridiculous about things and be together. Maybe it was just easier for teenagers to know what they wanted before the doubt of adulthood clouded their thinking with logic and rules. They better figure it out, Cara thought, or I am calling Grandma.

    Cara loved Noah and he loved her. They wanted to be together so every free chance they had, they were together. Cara realized when she was in Florida that Noah was her future. She decided then to take it slow. If he was truly the one for her, he would be understanding and would wait.

It was the conversations on the beach walks with William that made Cara realize that love, real love was so much more than just the sex the kids at school talked about. It was about respect and commitment. Cara felt that she and Noah were on the way to that place where they would be connected to each other for a long time. She didn't want to rush in to it, but rather savor every minute of the journey with him. At least in her heart she did but when they were together all she could think about was being in his arms skin to skin. Cara wondered if it was that way for her mom and William. She knew they didn't have sex, but did they crave to be next to each other? She knew her mom was wanting more with William. She also knew that marrying him scared her mother to death.

Cara looked up from the book she was reading as her mother walked through the living room headed to the kitchen. Her mother looked as if she had been crying. It was late and Cara had assumed that she had been asleep.

"Mom? What's up?" Cara asked.

Alison sat down across from her daughter in a comfy big chair. "I was talking to William. He is asking me about God again. The more we talk the more I feel he is going to give me an ultimatum. I'm not ready to lose him and I am not ready to admit to him how I feel about God when I don't really know that answer myself. I'm sorry I shouldn't be talking to you about William, dear."

"Mom, who else are you going to talk to? Really?" Cara said. "I do not care what you think about God but whatever you do, do not push William away. He is perfect for you and that man loves you."

"And I love him. Cara, I really do." She said sounding more like a lost little girl than a grown woman with an almost grown daughter.

"Then I do not understand what the problem is. Call him mother, tell him to come be with you. It is really that simple." Cara said. "Do I need to call him?" Both laughed. Cara continued. "Hey William, this is Cara your favorite Whovian, how about you come on back here now. My mother loves you and needs you in her life. Oh and in her bed though she won't admit that." Alison tossed a pillow at Cara.

"Don't you dare call him. I will call him tomorrow, I promise." Alison said. "Let's get some sleep, you silly girl."

Alison called William first thing the next morning. The phone rang repeatedly. Alison began to pace the floor. Finally, William answered.

"Alison what's wrong?"

"Hi William, nothing I…I'm fine." She said.

"No, you are not. I can feel your stress. Are you pacing the floor?" William said as he stopped his third trek across his living room.

"How could you possibly know I was…. never mind" Alison stopped and stood still shaking her head. "Listen William I called to tell you to come back to me. I can't go another day without you." After a few seconds of silence, Alison adds vehemently, "Please."

William smiled. "I just hung up with the pilot right before you called. I will be there in a few hours. I will come straight to your place. Do you work today?"

Alison smiled. "I quit my second job to spend time with Cara. I will call Fran and tell her I can't come in today. I want to be here when you get here."

"Ok, see you soon." William said and hang up without a response from Alison.

Alison did what she has always done when she was upset. She went and climbed in to her mother's bed. She snuggled down into the pale pink duvet and breathed in the smell of home. Elizabeth Lawson sat on the edge of the bed stroking her daughter's head. "Your babies are always your babies no matter how old or how they came in to your life." Elizabeth said.

"No truer words mom, that's for sure. I love Cara. She drives me insane, but I love her." Alison said.

Elizabeth chuckled. "Daughters do that, my love." Alison sighed, and Elizabeth continued. "For instance, I know you have the key to the old trunk in the attic."

Alison sheepishly buried her face in the covers. "Yea."

"I know you haven't looked in the trunk yet, so let's go do that together." Elizabeth said.

The two women went up into the attic. Alison worried as her mother went up the creaky stairs in front of her but stopped as soon as she saw Elizabeth pull the heavy trunk to the center of the dusty room. They both dropped to their knees and Alison reached in her pocket for her keys. The lock growled in protest and the dust stars sparkled under the light of one bulb that bobbed above them.

At first glance the trunk was filled with boxes of old cardboard boxes. Elizabeth reached in and pulled out a faded pink box. She held it like one would a fragile piece of glass. Alison held her breath as her mother ever so gently opened the box. Inside was a lacy sweet yellow baby dress with delicate smocking on the front scattered with tiny little pink flowers embroidered on the smocking. "You were so tiny when I first saw you. I was amazed at everything about you. You had perfect little fingers and toes." Elizabeth said more to the dress than to Alison. "When Ann placed you in my arms we both cried. I kissed your downy head." Confused Alison asked, "Who was Ann?"

Elizabeth looked up from the dress, her eyes glistened with unshed tears. "I will show you." She sat the dress aside and moved the other contents of the small faded box round until she came to a yellowed old photograph.

"This is Ann and me just a couple of days before you were born" Elizabeth handed the picture to Alison with a shaky hand. In the photo were to smiling women. One was dressed in a maternity dress that looked like it might have been blue, but the color of the photo had faded just like the pink box. Next to her was a second woman smiling just as wildly with her arm over the shoulders of the mother to be who was holding the woman's other hand in her lap.

The comprehension slid across Alison's face as she realized it was not her mother who was pregnant. Her mother was the smiling woman next to the obviously pregnant stranger sitting next to her. She tried to speak but no words formed in her mouth.

Elisabeth spoke in soft careful words, "I know you have tons of questions. For now, just know that I loved you from the moment I knew you were mine. I can't tell you anything about Ann other than her name and health history.

That was how things were done back then. I was lucky to have met her. It was her idea and we became instant friends. So my sweet Ally Cat, my love, when you think about the Gibsons and their crazy obsession with Cara, know that people will often stop at nothing to insure the safety and security of their children no matter how they came to be. Try not to be too hard on them but do not for a second let them push you out of her life."

Alison nodded. Her entire childhood flashed in technicolor images in her mind. She saw birthday parties, family outings and lazy days at home. She saw her dad and mom. Looking back, she could see no hint that she was adopted. Her life was as normal and American as a Norman Rockwell painting. She searched her thoughts for the questions, but surprisingly they didn't come. Somehow in her gut she knew she was raised by the parents God chose for her.

Chapter Twenty Eight

True to his word exactly three hours later William was standing on Alison's doorstep and she flung the door open before he could knock. He took two steps in to her house kicked the door closed behind him and tossed his hat on the coffee table.

William looked over at Alison who was smiling at him. He resisted the urge to snatch her up in his grasp and squeeze her hard. Instead he ran a finger down the side of her face, placed his palm on her face and his thumb on her chin lifting her face to his. "God I missed you." He said breathlessly into her mouth as he kissed her lightly then stronger.

After a few minutes he pulled away and looked into her eyes. He slowly dropped to one knee. "I was not going to propose this way, but damn it, I do not want to wait another second. Alison, marry me, today, now. If you want a fancy wedding with all the extravagant things women want, I will give you that later. I just can't go another day without you as my wife."

He held in his hands a white ring box with a gold KS embossed on the top. Alison recognized it as a ring box from Sabine Jewelry. She took the box into her shaking hand and slowly opened the box. Sitting on white velvet was a large deep green cushion cut stone surrounded by diamonds. William took the ring from the box and slid it on her ring finger.

"What do you say, my love?" William asked.

Alison said, "Yes" evenly and decisively. "Let's go get married."

William did not hesitate. In one motion, he scooped up his hat, placed it on his head, took Alison by the hand and headed out the door where Carl was waiting with the door to the limo open. Alison laughed as she got in the car. "How did you know I would say yes?"

"God told me you would be my wife." William said.

"God?" Alison looked terrified.

"No, don't you dare Alison. You can't tell me that you don't feel that this is the right thing to do." William said.

"Yes, yes." She said.

Alison climbed into the limo. She reached for her phone and called Cara's cell. It went straight to voicemail. Alison hung up without leaving a message.

William frowned, "We should wait for Cara."

"No" Alison said firmly. "My entire life has revolved around that child since the day she was born. I am not putting this off. She may get mad but we will let her plan a huge reception later. This moment, this day is about me and you." Alison paused, "if that is ok?"

"Certainly." William said.

The couple were married at the First Baptist Church of Savannah. The event lacked ceremony and lasted a whole of five minutes. The pastor said all the important parts and said a prayer over the couple. It was over so fast that Alison almost asked if they could do the entire thing again. They spent more time filling out the paperwork than they did actually getting married. When it came time for wedding rings William produced a second box out of a pocket from Sabine's with two simple wide matching silver wedding bands. Then it was down the front steps of the large white church.

    The pastor came striding out behind them. "Wait, you have to have at least one picture." Alison handed him her cell phone and he snapped a picture. As easy as that, she was Mrs. William Porter.

    Alison called Cara again, this she left a voicemail. "Hi Cara, I have great news. William is here and we got married. I know, it was sudden. Can't wait to tell you all about it. I may not be home tonight. Not sure where we are going but if you need me call my cell or William's. Be safe. On second thought let me hear from you."

The car maneuvered through the city. William could not take his eyes and his hands-off Alison. He caressed her hands, knees and arms. He kissed her lightly and then stared at her some more. Alison was so happy she thought she might burst however, she was self-conscience of the attention. She wondered where they were going, though she had an idea.

William, as if reading her thoughts, answered, out loud, "We are going to my room at the hotel."

Alison laughed. "Now?"

"Yes." William said smiling.

When the car pulled up at the hotel William got out, walked around to Alison's side of the car and opened the door. He held out his hand, "Get out."

Alison stammered, "But I don't have a bag, clothes, I don't even have a toothbrush."

"Shut up and get out of the car." William repeated.

Alison took his hand and got out of the car. She followed him into the hotel lobby. To her surprise they walked right past the hotel service desk to the elevator.

"Don't you need to..." she said started to say and pointed to the desk.

"Shush." William said. As soon as the elevator door closed he reached for her in big swoop of his arms and dipped her backwards. He smiled down at her and kissed her lightly on the lips.

The elevator stopped on the eighth floor and the doors opened. William stood Alison upright and held her hand. He pulled her out of the lift and down the corridor.

"No penthouse?" she asked.

"No, the bridal suite instead" he said.

He reached their room and slid the plastic key card into the reader and opened the door. He reached for her and lifted her in to his arms. She threaded her hands around his neck and buried her nose against his skin inhaling the scent that was him.

He gently set her feet on the floor after they had entered the room. Alison looked around and was surprised at how simple the room looked. She expected more luxury than a simple average hotel room. There was a rich comforter of deep forest green on the bed that was laden with decorative pillows of various shapes and sizes, but other than that it looked like any other hotel room. Over in one corner was a table set for two with a fruit and cheese tray. Next to the platter was a bottle of what looked like champagne on ice with two fluted glasses next to it. William poured them each a glass of the sparkling bubbly liquid gold. Alison looked confused.

"It's ok. It is nonalcoholic though I have been known to drink the occasional champagne. I didn't want to freak you out so soon after marrying you" he grinned.

She took the glass from him and he toasted to their future. After they clinked glasses she took a big gulp.

"That's too bad. I could use a drink to calm my nerves." She said cutting her eyes over to the bed. He smiled.

"Why are you nervous? You are not a virgin bride my dear."

"No, but it has been a long time, a really long time since a man has seen me without my clothes on. Even then" she sighed "I am embarrassed to say he didn't matter to me."

William stroked her shoulders and arms. "It's ok, love. Go in to the bathroom and get comfortable."

She nodded and did as she was told. In the bathroom was a robe of soft yellow silk. She took her clothes off, took a quick shower and put the robe on. When she came out of the bathroom she saw an undressed man in the bed covered with the sheet. His hat standing watch on the nightstand. She slipped in to the bed. She removed the robe after she was securely under the sheet. She noticed a drink next to the bed.

"Drink it." William said.

As she did she realized it was a sweet tasting whisky with a hint of apple. She gulped it down in two swallows. Setting the glass on the nightstand she settled down in to the bed.

William hovered over her and caressed her face with his hands. He wanted to take her right then in a rush of emotion; however, he knew he could not ravish her. It took every ounce if restraint not to climb on top of her and take what he wanted.

There was another side of him longing to take it slow and enjoy every inch of his new wife. She saw the conflict on his face. Her hand reached up and ran fingers through his hair. When her hand reached the back of his neck she pulled his head down to hers and kissed him fervently on the mouth letting her tongue delicately lick his lips. He moaned and lost himself in her. The passion rose within them and they kissed long and hungrily. Her hands traveled down his back and pulled him closer in to herself. He moved over her and placed his body between her legs.

"Are you ok?" he asked.

"Yes" came her soft reply. He kissed her breasts and slowly pushed in to her. The sensation sent him over the edge. He began to move, and she responded in mirrored motion.

Alison felt her love for William expand in her as he whispered her name. She began to shudder in climax and in a matter of moments he followed her.

They spent the afternoon exploring each other. It was easy as if they had known each other for a lifetime, yet it was new at the same time. They spoke very little. No declarations of love were spoken by either of them. They did not need the words. Love was all around them. Flowing between them like an unseen force. Their bodies fit together seamlessly as if they were made from one mold. There was not awkwardness or clumsy hands. There was only the skilled moves of experience that guided them.

Afterwards, spent and exhausted, they entangled in each other's embrace, William asked, "Now tell me, did I run away when I saw you nude?"

Alison shook her head.

"Did you enjoy being with me?" he asked.

She nodded, blushed and ducked her head on to his chest. "I am not going anywhere. You are safe with me. We are just getting started, Mrs. Porter." William said. "Sleep well, my love."

Chapter Twenty Nine

Lauren decided to not try to sweeten the long difficult road that was her past. She had to tell Mark all of it and tell him the truth. She had to tell him that it wasn't just her life that was twisted in secrecy and anguish but that of William Porter's friend, Alison.

Lauren was praying that when William gave her the name of the girl he wanted information on that there were two women named Alison Lawson in Savannah. She was hoping against hope that it wasn't the same one who she knew to have a baby with Lance Gibson. Once she looked at the cafe's website, found the Meet the Staff page and saw a photo of Alison she knew it was the same woman with the same daughter. How would she tell Mark or

William the truth? Lauren did not have that answer but she knew that she must be honest if she was to have may sort of future with the man she loved.

Lauren and Mark had taken a break from the conversation to get a shower and have something to eat. They were sitting on the sofa and Mark was looking at her expectantly waiting for her to resume telling her story. Just as she was about to begin Mark's phone rang. He knew that it was William before he looked at the screen. Mark raised an eyebrow at Lauren and indicated that he had to answer the call. She nodded.

"Hello, boss." Mark said. "Yes, I am here with Lauren." Mark put the phone on speaker and rested it on the sofa between them. "Go ahead sir she can hear you. The speaker is on."

"Hi, well I am at the hotel in Savannah and Alison is here. She is sleeping in the other room. I have to tell you both that I proposed to her." William said.

Both Mark and Lauren began to give their congratulations, but William stopped them. "Wait there is more. I married her today as well." Lauren and Mark looked at each other blinking for several seconds.

"Hello?" came William's voice from the phone.

"We are here sir. I am surprised." Mark said, "Happy for you boss, but surprised."

William chuckled. "Lauren, please tell Mark whatever info you have on Alison. If it is important Mark, you will decide if I need to know it or not. I need you to understand. I do not care what dark or nasty skeletons you find in her past. She is my wife. If it is something I can live the rest of my life without needing to know, then so be it. I will not change my mind about her. I love her. She is mine."

"Sir isn't this putting the cart before the preverbal horse?" Mark asked.

Yes, maybe." William said but did not continue.

Lauren sighed. Her mind was racing.

"Ok sir. Goodbye." Mark said and disconnected the call.

"Wow" Lauren said.

"I am so sorry dear. Can you hold your story and go get the info you have on Alison please?" Mark asked her.

"Well that is the thing Mark. My story involves her." Lauren said. Mark looked confused.

"What do you mean?" He asked.

"Alison Lawson is part of my sister's past." Lauren said. "Though they never met."

"I think you need to explain. That woman is now married to William." Mark said getting agitated.

"Just listen." Lauren said. "After my mom's party when my sister announced to the world she was pregnant, my sister told us that she had a one-night stand with a guy in the some dorm as Charles. That guy was Lance Gibson."

Mark was stunned for the second time in less than a half hours' time. "Lauren, please tell me the rest of the story." Marks said evenly. Lauren was petrified. She took a deep breath and began to speak anyway.

Lauren explained how Marion sent Traci to a girl's home close to Atlanta. Plans were made to give her baby up for adoption the instant it was born. The adoption never happened. The baby was stillborn. "My mother was relieved. Mark, I was secretly relieved too." Lauren said, "Does that make me a bad person?"

"No, love, it makes you human" Mark answered. Lauren sighed.

"My sister never really got over it. She grieved for a long time."

"How does this have anything to do with Alison?" Mark asked.

"Well, besides the fact my sister's baby and Alison's daughter have the same father?" Lauren said a little sharper than she meant too.

"Yes, what aren't you telling me?" he pushed.

"Alison was sent to the same home for pregnant girls." Lauren said.

"I know there is more, I can see it all over you Lauren." Mark said.

Laurens nodded. "Yes Mark there is more."

Chapter Thirty

William and Alison walked in to the modest mobile home. Alison looked around at an immaculate room. The floor had been recently vacuumed, there was no sign of teenage laziness anywhere. There were no dishes left over from a late-night snack on the coffee table. Even Cara's fashion magazines were in a neat stack on the said table. Alison walked in to the kitchen and there wasn't a single dirty plate or cup to be seen. "Amazing." Alison said under her breath.

William looked concerned. He headed down the hall and then back to where Alison was standing with her hands on her hips. He shook his head. Just then Alison's phone rang.

"Hi Cara." Alison answered.

"Hi, is that all you can say? Married!" Cara said.

"About that?" Alison said looking over at William sheepishly.

"I am so happy for you! Where are you?" Cara asked.

"Home. The house looks good by the way."

"Mother! Where is William and why aren't you on a honeymoon on the beach someplace?" Cara chastised.

Alison laughed, "He is here. We will do the honeymoon thing later. We haven't figured out all the details yet. I am so glad you aren't mad."

"How could I be mad?" Cara said. "I am going to stay at my friend Cathy's house for a couple of days ok? You guys need honeymoon time."

"Sure, and Cara. "Alison continued. "Stay away from the Gibson's please."

"I can't promise that mom." Cara said. "Don't worry. Enjoy married life how about that? I love you mom. Please don't worry." Cara disconnected the call.

"Everything alright?" William asked taking her into his embrace.

"She seems ok. I just don't know William," Alison said shaking her head.

He hugged his bride tight.

"It will be ok. God has Cara just like he has us." William said.

"If you say so Mr. Porter." Alison conceded.

Chapter Thirty One

Lauren finally got up the nerve to tell Mark the rest of the story. They were sitting on the balcony of Lauren's apartment drinking wine. He was searching through documents doing research on some secret project that Lauren did not know a thing about. She honestly did not want to know. She remembered how serious things got when Mark and William were researching a case. As if he read her thoughts Mark's forehead scrunched up and got all lined across the surface. Lauren stood up behind his chair and began to squeeze his shoulders. He groaned and on cue removed his shirt so she could lightly scratch his back.

"Hum, what are you doing to me love?" he asked.

"Trying to distract you from your work." She replied.

"Well how about distract us both by telling me the rest of your story." Mark said. He wanted to encourage her but not push her to hard. He already had an idea of what happened. "I can do that. I need to finish it." Lauren took a deep breath. "Let's go inside."

Bartons decided to go to the lake house to spend a few days. It is far away from normal life. The family made their way down the quarter mile private driveway to the parking area that was conveniently located directly outside the front door. As they entered through the front door, there was a full bath with shower on the left and a bedroom with queen size bed to the right. Just ahead there was the great room, with a grand stone wood burning fireplace, cathedral ceilings, expensive furnishings, and a television.

The kitchen was open to the great room. Just around the corner from the kitchen was the laundry room with unique tile flooring with small yellow tiles in the shape of ducklings. A table was located next to the kitchen and the island are convenient for meal time adjacent to a screened in porch with a second wood fireplace.

"My parents were hoping that staying at the lake would give Traci time to recoup over what happened with the baby." Lauren continued. "It didn't happen."

"What did happen?" Mark prompted.

Lauren sighs and fidgets on the sofa. Mark pats her leg and gets up. He makes his way to the kitchen and pours Lauren and himself a glass of wine. He hands one to her and smiles.

"Darling if we are going to be married, successfully married, we need to establish right now that we are always going to be honest with each other. I want us to have kids one day and rule number one in our house will be always be honest. How can we expect our children to be honest with us if we are not honest with each other?" He took her face in his hands and kissed her. "I am not going to force you to tell me anything, but I am not going to tolerate lies. I can promise you I can lie but I will never lie to you." Mark said as he leaned back away from Lauren.

"That is not unreasonable." Lauren said. "Here is the thing Mark. My sister's baby did not die." Confusion spread across Mark's face. Lauren continued softly, "The Gibson's paid an unethical doctor to switch the babies."

"What do you mean switch the babies? Who's baby?" Mark attempted to wrap his brain around what Lauren was trying to explain. Lauren sighed and tried again. "Alison Lawson's baby was still born. The Gibson's switched my sisters living baby for Alice Lawson's dead baby. Cara Lawson is a Barton and a Gibson by blood."

Mark was stunned. He took a deep breath.

"A Barton?" Mark asked.

Lauren nodded.

"Cara is not Alison's child?"

Lauren nodded again.

"Do you realize what this means?" Mark said more to himself than to her.

Lauren nodded once again.

"Why would the Gibson's do that? If Lance is the biological father of both babies why would they switch the mothers? It makes no sense." Mark stood and began to pace the floor. "I am assuming that Alison and Cara do not know all this?"

"No one knows now but me. Well me, Paula and Lance Gibson." Lauren admitted. "I stumbled across the truth after it was too late to stop the plan."

"I have to go. I have to tell William." Mark began to look for his car keys.

"Wait, Mark!" Lauren panicked. "You can't."

"Why not?" Mark looked at her and Lauren could see the anger start to boil in his face.

"Because the Gibson's have the power to ruin me." Lauren replied. "It's because of me that my sister is dead."

Chapter Thirty Two

"Where will we live?" an agitated Alison asked William as she rested her head on his shoulder and rubbed his chest with her hand. The afternoon light pouring in the window of her bedroom bouncing glimmers of green off the emerald on her left hand. A soft hum came from an almost asleep William.

"Shush, we will worry about that later" he murmured.

Alison sat up. It had been three days of romance, relaxing and sex for the newlyweds and the spell was wearing off as Alison began to worry about the practicality of what they had done.

"William, we need to figure this out. You and I both have jobs to get back too." Alison looked down at his smiling face and closed eyes.

"William? Are you listening?"

"Yes, love, I hear every word and you need to relax. We will be fine." He said as he wrapped her in an embrace and pulled her back down in to him.

"How can you not be concerned about all the practical stuff we need to work out?" She asked him.

"Because I trust God. He has it worked out for us and it will all be fine." William reached for her and kissed her softly. His hand smacked her on the backside. "Now go get a shower so we can head out for dinner. What do you want to eat? That is all you need to worry about right now."

Alison got up exasperated. "Fine, just fine."

They walked into the diner to an explosion of applause. All of the wait staff including Fran hugged them offering best wishes and congratulations. Alison was overwhelmed and dabbed tears from her eyes. She looked up and realized there were no customers at any of the tables. "What is happening?" she asked Fran who waited to be the last one to greet the couple.

"Well, we wanted to give you a surprise since we weren't invited to the wedding." The older woman said just as the kitchen door swung open and two bus boys wheeled out a cart holding a huge four-tiered ivory wedding cake with a figurine if a woman pulling a cowboy by the shirt collar holding a shotgun in her other hand. Alison looked at William who noticed the topper too and was laughing a deep loud belly laugh.

"That is the funniest thing I have seen in a long time." He said. Alison relaxed then.

The afternoon went on with Alison's friends, including Faith coming and going. Even Alison's mother Elizabeth came to wish her new son in law a long happy marriage to her daughter.

"I guess my home cooked meal idea worked." She jokingly said when she hugged Alison.

William said "Yes, yes it did. I can't let cooking skills like that get away from me. I knew I had to marry her." The older woman laughed as Alison elbowed him teasingly.

"Oh no, it must have been my dating a Christian man advice that did the trick." Faith chimed in.

"It was both." Alison conceded.

"So where will you two live?" Alison's mother asked.

"Well mother funny you should ask. I will let William answer that." Alison tried not to smirk at William who was still grinning. He had not removed the smile from his face since they arrived at the diner.

"We haven't worked it all out yet, but Alison's place is too tiny for a big guy like me." He looked over at Alison as if to say, take that.

Chapter Thirty Three

Alison was glad that William decided to stay a bit longer in Savannah. William called and asked her to spend the following weekend at the hotel with him. She drove herself over to the hotel after she got home from work and showered. She put on her favorite yellow dress, the one William had bought for her in Florida. She even treated herself to a manicure. Her hair was shining down her back in a loose braid. She looked young and happy. She realized she was happy. She knew that no matter what happened between her and William Porter that she would never be alone. God was there with her and she was happy. This happy was a strange thing. Even when the day was rough at work and she was stressed, she was still happy. She still felt happiness in her heart and she smiled through the stress. It was amazing.

Alison entered the lobby and the doorman took her bags.

"Hello, shall I ring Mr. Porter's room for you?" he asked.

"No, he knows I am on my way."

"Very well. I will take your bag up." He said.

"Thank you." She entered the elevator and pushed the button for the correct floor. She was surprised at how nervous she was to see William. Her knees were shaking. Weird. The evaluator chimed and the doors opened. Alison looked up to a waiting Mark.

"Hi Mark. I thought you had gone back to Florida." She said.

"I was called back here on an urgent task." Mark said, "This way please."

Mark lead Alison down the hall and past the door to the living room of the suite.

"Wait, where are we going?" she asked confused.

Mark opened the door to a staircase and motioned for her to walk up the stairs. He followed behind her. When they reached the top, the door opened to the roof garden of the hotel. William was standing there with his back to Alison. She approached him slowly and evenly.

William turned around and looked her straight in the eyes. He held up a hand and she stopped frozen in her steps. "Alison, I need to tell you something. It is not easy and it is not good." William motions to her to sit on a nearby sofa while he remained standing. Alison sits. "I found out that Cara has decided to continue to see Lance and is considering changing her last name to Gibson. Also, she is going to go on a vacation with them soon. She has been hiding it from you because she doesn't want you to be hurt."

Alison put her face in her hands. "I thought we were doing so much better. We are talking and spending more time together. Even her grades are up." Alison looked up at William her face white.

"The Gibsons have my Cara?" Alison whispered. "I tried to call her but she isn't answering her phone. She told me she was spending the night with a friend from school but I had a feeling she was up to something. To be honest I thought she was with Noah"

"Alison how long has she been gone?" he asked her.

"Yesterday. I waited up all night and I figured she would come home. She didn't so I went to work. I don't know what to do." She said. William walked over to her, sat down and stroked her cheek wiping the wet tracks off her face.

"I will tell you just what you will do my sweet smart beautiful woman. We will go over to the Gibson's place and remind them of the agreement that they are breaking by doing whatever it is with Cara. We will also remind them it was their idea in the first place to stay away from her. I will not allow you to be their doormat any longer Alison Porter." William proclaimed as he stood up and straightened his hat on his head. "Now, let's go get our daughter."

They rode in the back of the limo in silence. Alison had given Carlos Lance Gibson's address off the top of her head, which surprised her. She remembered everything about him, even his house number. Alison remembered the way it felt to have him hold her and tell her he loved her. She knew that what she and Lance had together was not love. It was an obsession that would hurt everyone close to them and it was over. Alison was finally finished with Lance once and for all. She reached over and opened up the mini bar. "I need a drink." She said. She reached for a miniature bottle of vodka and a small can of orange juice. She poured them both in a glass and drank it in a couple of gulps. Wiping her mouth with the back of her hand she reached in and snatched up a second bottle.

"Are you sure you want to do that?" William asked.

"Listen you deal with stress your way and I will deal with it mine. I need all the help I can get. You do not know what we are up against here. These people are brutal. They could have you and me arrested on some trumped up shit charge with one phone call." Alison said. She realized that she had just used profanity that used to come out of her mouth so easily but had stopped since she married William. "I'm sorry. I tend to get a potty mouth when I drink, and it doesn't take much."

William patted her hand. "I have been known to let a few slips too."

The car stopped outside the huge brown stone and Alison was wishing she had a better plan than just show up and say hey give me my moody teenager back. William and she walked

There and Back   Lori O'Gara

up to the door and she hesitated with her finger in the air above the doorbell button. William moved her hand out of the way and he rang the bell. An older tall man opened the door. "May I help you?" he said.

"Yes, I am William Porter and this is my wife. We have reason to believe that our daughter Cara Lawson is here. Again. We want to speak to her now." William said.

"This way sir and madam," said the man motioning to them to come in to the house.

Alison and William followed him to a sitting room with blue furniture. Neither one of them sat.

What can I do for you, Mr. Porter? I do not believe we have officially met." Paula said as she entered the room.

"I am here for my daughter." Alison said looking over at William " Our daughter." Alison saw a white face Lance Gibson was staring back at her from over his wife's shoulder.

"What are you doing here? I believe that Cara made her feelings very clear Alison. She wants to live with me." He said smugly.

"I do not give a damn what that sixteen-year-old little girl wants. I am her mother and she is coming home to me." Alison exploded. "Where is she?"

"I am not letting you take her Alison." Lance said defiantly.

In a flash, Alison pulled out the hand gun and pointed it at Lance's chest. "Are you sure about that?"

"Mom, what are you doing?" Cara yelled from the stairway in the hall. Alison pushed past Paula and Lance in to the foyer.

"You are coming home. Now." Alison said looking up at her daughter.

"Is that a gun? Since when do you have a gun?" Cara asked terrified.

"Since always, now go pack your things. I am you mother and you are coming with me." Alison said.

Lance Gibson moved in between Alison and the foot of the stairs. "Alison please be reasonable. We can make some sort of arrangement that works for everyone."

"Like the last arrangement?" Alison hissed "She is my daughter and I am taking her home."

"Oh mom, please let's talk first." Cara pleaded. "I need to speak with you."

"Cara we can go home and talk there." Alison demanded. "No mom. We can't. Everything I have to say can be said right here. Put the stupid gun down." Cara took a step toward Alison.

Lance also took a step toward Alison. She lifted the gun. "No Lance, I am not making any arrangements with you and your family's money. When Cara is eighteen she can do as she pleases until then she is living in my house and I am taking care of her."

William walked up behind Alison. "Allie, put the gun down love. You won't fix anything by putting a bullet in that man."

Alison's hands began to shake and she steadied herself. Her hands stopped shaking. An elegant woman appeared on the landing behind Cara. She was tall, slim and beautiful. She placed a hand on Cara's shoulder and peered down the stairs where William and Alison were standing. William looked at her and blinked. "Listen to him Alison, *love*." The woman sneered. "William Porter doesn't toss that word, the all-powerful word love around lightly."

"What the hell are you doing here, Evette?" William said moving from behind Alison to stand squarely in front of her.

"Oh, that's right, William darling. You knew me as a Johnson not as my married name, Gibson. I am married to Lance's older brother, Steve." Evette said. "Good to see you, William."

There and Back   Lori O'Gara

"Come on Alison, we need to get out of here. Put the gun down and let's go, now." William said ignoring the woman on the stairs. Alison looked up at Evette Gibson and then back at William.

"How do you know her?" Alison questioned William.

"Alison remember the story I told you about the woman?" Alison nodded slowly.

"Evette is that woman." He said flatly "Now, let's go."

"Not without my daughter." Alison hissed.

William looked up at Cara in a questioning look. Cara shook her head defiantly. "I can't believe you would come here with a damn gun." Cara stomped back up the stairs. Alison walked closer to Lance. "If you ever try to take her from me again. I will unload this gun into you. I will have nothing to lose, she is all I have in this world Lance and you know that. Leave her alone."

Cara appeared and came down the stairs. "Mother, you will not keep me from the Gibson's especially Lance. You can't now that I know the truth."

"I don't know what truth you think you know Cara." Cara continued ignoring her mother.

"The truth is that I am a Gibson and Lance is my father, but you mom, you are not my mother."

"What are you talking about Cara? I birthed you." Alison looked at Paula and Lance "What kind of poison have you been spilling in her brain."

"It's the truth." Said Paula flatly. "We switched the babies."

William's face sank. He did not want Alison to hear the awful truth this way. "Stop, this is not the way we need to discuss this. Not here not like this." Alison spun on her heels and faced William.

"What are you talking about William?" Alison said through clenched teeth.

Just then the door opened behind them and stoic Mark with Lauren entered the hall way. Mark handed William a manila envelope. William pulled out the paper and handed it to Alison. It was a copy of a death certificate and a birth certificate. Alison scanned the documents. She looked more confused.

"Who is Traci Barton?" Alison asked.

"My sister, she was my sister." said Lauren timidly. Lauren took Alison by the hand and led her to the sitting room. She did not attempt to take the gun from her.

"Can you lay the gun there on the table please?" said Lauren in her distinct soft librarian tone. Alison did as she requested.

William and Mark began to enter the room. Lauren lifted a palm to stop them and shook her head. They backed out and waited. Lauren explained to Alison in soft even tones what she knew, and Mark had discovered.

"There was a baby girl born three days after Cara and she died. My sister Traci was told her baby died. It was a lie. Somehow the Gibson's orchestrated the entire thing. They swapped my sisters health baby girl with the dead baby. Alison, your baby." Lauren paused to see if Alison was following her.

"What?" Alison said barley over a whisper. "How is that even possible? I saw Cara. I saw her when she came out of me." Alison closed her eyes trying to remember exactly what Cara looked like then. "She was beautiful, she didn't cry but..."

Lauren continued. "They counterfeited the documents. The ones you have in your hands are those documents."

"Wait a damn second. How could the Gibson's even know about your sister?" Alison questioned.

"My sister was sent to college in Atlanta. Didn't you have Cara in Atlanta?" Lauren asked and Alison nodded. "My sister was a wild girl.

There and Back   Lori O'Gara

She had one night stands all the time. One night she got drunk and ended up in bed with Lance. Her fiancé, Charles dumped her when he found out. She was desperate. She realized Lance Gibson had money and she tried to extort him. Not wanting yet another pregnant girl to deal with they swapped the babies and told Traci that her baby died."

Alison was shaking. "Why? Why not just tell us both the babies died and get rid of both of us? It makes no sense."

"I don't know what they were thinking." Lauren said. "I am so sorry Alison but it is the truth."

"I can tell you why we saved Cara." Paula Gibson came in to the room. "Lance wanted a child and you were the most manipulable girl in the equation. What we didn't count on was that old man Gibson would cut Lance off from the family fortune if he had any baby. As an alternative, we came up with the arrangement with you in the hopes that Lance would find a loophole and get to keep his money and his daughter. You were the easiest one to deal with. Traci Barton was bat shit crazy and volatile."

Lauren rose to stand toe to toe with Paula Gibson. She reached up and slapped the woman hard in the face. "My sister is dead because of you and your lies." Lauren hissed. "She never got over the loss of her child. She committed suicide."

"This, this conversation, this house is crazy. I am getting out of here with my child." Alison said and with one smooth motion she swiped up the gun from the table and pushed past Lauren and a stunned Paula.

Cara was coming down the stairs. Lance took two long strides toward the stairs. William sensed the shift in Alison's stance before she moved. William reached for her and the gun. The loud obnoxious sound sliced through the foyer shaking the air and swung the chandelier. Time stood still freezing everyone where they stood. There was a scream. Was it Cara? William thought. The light of the room began to close in on William as he fell at Alison's feet. Silence surrounded them, as if even the house was holding its breath.

Alison dropped to her knees as a thick puddle of blood formed around William. She held his head in her lap. She stroked his hair and his face. She tried to say she was sorry, that it was an accident but no words formed in her mouth. He looked up at her, but his eyes are empty and dull. The shrill rhythmic sound of a siren on the distance made the bystanders move.

Paula opens the door and steps out watching for the police and the ambulance. Cara begins to cry. Evette watches over the railing from her perch on the landing. Alison continues to hold William rocking his heavy head back and forth. She stays by his side as the first responders began to rip his shirt off his body revealing the wet hole in his chest. It was only when Lance's arms reached around Alison and pulled her away from William did the words bolt out of her. "William! William!....I love you!" She screamed as sobs shook her body. She fought to get close to him again hitting Lance and kicking him trying to get free. In a matter of seconds William was gone. He was in the ambulance. The ambulance was barreling down the road toward the hospital.

    Alison was alone in a room full of enemies.

Chapter Thirty Four

The summer breeze was soft against Lauren's face as she lay on a blanket by the coast her journal lay loosely in her hands. Above her head the piercing screech from the sea gulls and their choppy melody trickled down to her. Lauren looked up at the crystal blue sky as clouds floated by in white fluffy splendor. She sighed long and deep. I wish summer lasted forever, she thought. She looked down at her journal at the scrawled words she had written and read them out loud. "I want to escape from my family and my sick sad sister."

Suddenly Lauren hears a piercing gut wrenching cream, she jumps and runs into the beach house. She runs up the porch steps and snatches the screen door open in one swift movement. That is when she hears her father and mother wailing upstairs. She takes the steps two at a time. Stumbling in her mad rush to get to her family. She collides in to Fred at the top of the landing. He is ashen and seizes Lauren by the arm and tries to force her back down the stairs. "Dad? What has Traci done now?" Lauren said as she pulled from her father. He shakes his head and Lauren pushes past him. The scent of hot steamed roses fills her nose. Lauren loathed the rose scented soap that Traci insisted using religiously. It reminded her of the overpowering perfume the old ladies at church wore.

  Lauren rounded the corner in to the bathroom. It was filled with mist from the scalding water. Marion is sitting on the floor next to the bathtub. Traci's wet head is in her mother's lap as Marion's hand loving strokes the wet tendrils off her face. Traci is naked and not moving. Lauren looks over into the tub and sees the empty pill bottle floating on the water as it slips under a pile of iridescent bubbles. Lauren jolts awake.

It takes a few minutes for Lauren to realize she had been dreaming. The steady beep of the monitors reminded her where she was. She looked over to the other chair where Mark sat his face in his hand asleep as well. She focused her eyes on the bed and saw that there was no change to William. He was still unconscious with an exhausted Alison laying over with her head on his arm. Her hand stroking his. Her emerald and wedding band sparkling. The room was silent all but the whoosh whirl of the respirator and the beep of the monitor that Alison would not let the nurses mute.

Lauren knew better than to suggest that Alison go get a cup of coffee much less go home to shower and rest. She had tried that and Alison all but attacked her for it. Lauren knew that William's dear friends Krystal and Brendan Dario would be there soon. She hoped that maybe then Alison would take a few moments to get some rest and some nourishment.

As if on cue Krystal and Brendan walk in with Brendan carrying a drink holder with three cups of coffee. He shook Mark's hand and gave him a cup, then passed one over to Lauren. He inclined his head toward Alison and Lauren shook her head indicating no, she hasn't moved.

Krystal walked over and put her hands on to Alison's shoulders. Ever so softly, as a mother speaks to a baby, Krystal said to Alison, "Come on darling, let's get some coffee in you." A red rim set of eyes look up from Alison to Krystal.

"I can't leave him." Alison said in a barely audible whisper.

"I am not asking you to leave him, just stand and let us take care of you. You know damn good and well William will be mad as a Tennessee rooster if he finds out I didn't take care of his girl."

"Oh, Krystal, he can't leave me." Alison whimpers as waves of sorrow shake her but no tears fall. She is out of tears from nonstop crying.

"That is not up to you my sweet friend. That is between William and God. If I know William he won't leave easily." Krystal said.

"I hope not. If he goes I am going with him." Alison manages to say as the sobs start again.

"Be strong, Alison. Do not be afraid; do not be discouraged, God will be with you wherever you and William go."

Epilogue

William Porter

I have a love hate relationship with the Almighty. I love him with all my heart and I hate myself when I knowingly avoid doing what he has set out for me to do. I know that he wants me to go find the answers and bring them back to her. She needs to know the truth. The man she loves is not dead. He is alive and I have found him. I know if I bring the answers back that I will lose her forever. I do not want to risk that, but God spoke. He said clearly, "She is not yours to keep. I have a woman for you."

All I feel is pain. Searing pain flowing through me like a hot knife. As quickly as it started it is gone. I was acutely aware of the light that surrounded me. I felt the warmth before I opened my eyes and saw it. It was as if I was standing in the middle of the sun and not getting burned up. I was in the furnace with the three men in the book of Daniel. The light pure white was all around me. Peace, perfect peace. I wanted to stay but I wanted to go back to her. I knew she was far away.

I woke suddenly. It was a dream. I was laying in the bed with Alison. Her even breaths of sleep came from her as she in her own dream lay with her head on my shoulder. I look down at her as she starts to stir. She sleepily looks up at me and smiles. In a flash, I am all alone in and empty bed with an annoying sound chiming on and on……off someplace close but far at the same time. Where is that sound coming from? Its relentless bleeping matches the rhythm of my heart. God make it stop, I beg.

"Not yet my son. I am not done with you. Not yet."

About the Author

Lori O'Gara is happiest with her feet in the sugar white sand on the coast of the Gulf of Mexico. She grew up on Perdido Key, Florida and currently resides with her childhood sweetheart just a few miles from where they grew up. She will be the first to admit that she is addicted to books. She doesn't always read what is on the bestseller list. She likes romance novels with a magical spin and memoirs about everyday people. Lori's literary philosophy is simple. Read what you like. If you can't read through the first couple of chapters without your mind wandering to other things in your life or if you dread having to finish it, then throw it out the front door. (No tossing a library book please.) Read what speaks to your heart. When not writing or reading Lori can be found wandering the stacks of her library, watching Doctor Who or spending time with her family.

Look for these books in the Perdido Key Series

The Perdido Key Novels

We Will Get There
Almost There
There and Back
Away From There
Never There

There and Back   Lori O'Gara

Made in the USA
Columbia, SC
15 September 2021